LYDIA'S FUNERAL VIDEO

a solo play

LYDIA'S FUNERAL VIDEO

a solo play

by
SAM CHANSE

KAYA PRESS
LOS ANGELES
NEW YORK

For information about permission to reproduce selections from this book,
please write to permissions@kaya.com.

Published by Kaya Press
www.kaya.com

Cover and book design by spoon+fork
Illustrations by Matt Huynh

Distributed by D.A.P./Distributed Art Publishers
155 Avenue of the Americas, 2nd Floor, New York, NY 10013
800.338.BOOK www.artbook.com

ISBN: 9781885030085

Library of Congress Control Number: 2015002529
Chanse, Samantha.
Lydia's funeral video : a solo play / by Sam Chanse.
    pages cm
ISBN 978-1-885030-08-5
I. Title.
PS3603.H35755L93 2015
812'.6--dc23

Printed in the United States of America

This publication is made possible by support from the USC Dana and
David Dornsife College of Arts, Letters, and Sciences; the USC Department
of American Studies and Ethnicity; and the USC Asian American Studies
Program. Kaya Press is funded in part by the Los Angeles Board of
Supervisors through the Los Angeles County Arts Commission. Special thanks
to the Choi Chang Soo Foundation for their support of this work. Additional
funding was provided through the generous contributions of Lily & Tom
Beischer, Lisa Chen & Andy Hsiao, Floyd & Sheri Cheung, Jim Chu, Prince
Gomolvilas, Jean Ho, Huy Hong, Juliana S. Koo, Whakyung Lee, Ed Lin, Noriko
Murai, Viet Thanh Nguyen, Gene & Sabine Oishi, Chez Bryan Ong, Thaddeus
Rutkowski, Anantha Sudhakar, Patricia Miye Wakida, Duncan Williams, Amelia
Wu & Sachin Adarkar, Anita Wu & James Spicer, and others.

CONTENTS

LYDIA'S FUNERAL VIDEO

INTRO **7**

ACT ONE **11**

ACT TWO **55**

ACT THREE **125**

NOTES **145**

AFTERWORD

EYE CONTACT **151**

LYDIA'S FUNERAL VIDEO

EDITORIAL NOTES

Translating live performances into printed matter often offers unique challenges. For *Lydia's Funeral Video*, we wrestled with the question of what is lost in such a translation—that is, the specificity and nuance of performance, particularly how the performer inhabits and expresses each of the multiple, distinct characters in the piece—and how the lived performance might be effectively re-imagined and interpreted into book form. Rather than try to recreate the *exact* experience of the performance, we decided instead to try to create an *analogous* experience. What, using print and page, could we do to capture some of the nuances of character and emotion that an audience member would pick up in a live performance but that becomes unavailable to the reader of a book?

After a fair amount of experimentation, we arrived at two new elements that are integral to this book: the counterpoint narrative and the illustrations.

The counterpoint narrative (CPN) lives in the bottom margins of the text, and offers a kind of running commentary throughout. The narrator of the CPN is unidentified, but the voice and perspective suggest someone with an intimate understanding of Lydia's psychological and emotional landscape—territory that Lydia herself is not necessarily always consciously aware of. There's no correct way that these notes are meant to interact with the text. Rather, they're meant to provide some additional information that readers can choose to access or not as desired.

The illustrations are meant to feel associative and improvisatory—the doodling of someone who has been pulled into the story, who is participating in the story, and who is drawing in a subconscious, train-of-thought fashion.

These two elements, in concert with the more familiar stage directions, are used throughout the book. While neither the CPN nor the illustrations replaces the experience of a live performance, they can, and we hope do, interact with the written text of the play to form another resonant incarnation of the piece.

Additional notes: Punctuation is sometimes used to convey rhythm and delivery.

Also, some of the light and sound design elements described in the stage directions are records of earlier productions, and are included here to provide readers with one possible expression of the visual and sound world of the show.

PLACE

The San Francisco Bay Area.

TIME

The not-so-distant future.

CHARACTERS

(PERFORMED BY A SINGLE PERFORMER)

Lydia Clark-Lin

A career bank clerk who secretly haunts standup comedy open mics. Late twenties; mixed Asian/Caucasian.

Bubbly

A figure in Lydia's dreams. Speaks slowly and strangely, with a childlike yet authoritative voice; no sense of humor at all. Represented by Lydia's hand(s), then by light globules.

Bernadette Tayag

A celebrity abortion doctor, founder of Family Planning Mobile Services (FPMS), and Lydia's childhood friend. Early thirties; Filipina American.

Cynthia Clark-Lin

A TV reporter with Greater Halifax News, and Lydia's semi-estranged mother. Late fifties, looks younger; white.

Kimmie

Lydia's sweet, ebullient banking co-worker. She means well.

Gin

The co-creator of Lydia's developing embryo, I.T. geek, and someone else's fiancé; 30s.

Host

A host at a weekly comedy open mic.

Lindsey Gough

Co-chair of a citizens' activist group; indeterminate older age.

INTRO

INTRO

In darkness, we recognize the sounds of a busy coffee house: the hissing of an espresso machine, the clattering of ceramic dishes, conversations being carried on at low and not-so-low murmurs.

Gradually, we see a microphone stand in a tight pool of light.

LYDIA CLARK-LIN cautiously approaches the microphone. Her posture is reflexively defensive, her movements tentative, but she is fueled by neurotic energy.

She glances at the audience members with anxiety.

The anxiety, however, is controlled, to a degree.

She glances down at a thin stack of index cards in her hands.

The sounds of the café diminish, but continue.

Finally, she speaks:

Hi.

My name is Lydia Clark-Lin and I am here against my will, under orders from my developing fetus, who visits me in my sleep and gives me instructions.

> She looks around the room, taking in the blank stares.

(moving on quickly, this can still work out) Um, okay, so I anticipated that if I introduced myself in that way, I might receive this kind of response, so I guess that's okay.

I mean, I'm kidding, anyway. I don't have a developing fetus talking to me, that would be, like, *crazy*, right?

It's an embryo, technically. Until the eighth week.

And, don't worry, it's not gonna make it that long!

> She checks in with the audience.
>
> Hmm. Not too encouraging; the outlook is grim.
>
> She freezes and the café sounds and lights cut out.

ACT ONE

THE NOT-SO-DISTANT FUTURE.
DAYS 3 – 8.

ACT ONE

SCENE 1

....

Lydia's San Francisco apartment.
Day 3.

....

The voice of a somewhat panicked LYDIA emerges from the unlit stage.

Maybe the apocalypse will come tomorrow.

As the lights rise, Lydia is revealed moving about the stage, adjusting furniture in relation to an unseen camera that she glances at occasionally, and muttering to herself.

Why am I doing this? I can't believe I'm doing this...(searching on a remote control) **power button, power button...where is power button... technology hard...**

She grumbles, but goes along anyway.

As if she has no choice.

ACT ONE   (fumbling) **Okay, Lydia. Video camera, *on.***

> Sitting down on the couch, she points the remote at an unseen camera.
>
> The lights bump up.
>
> A moment passes as she confronts the camera. She's clearly not in the habit of addressing these things, but she's giving it a shot, why not? She's adventurous. Sort of.

Hello.

Welcome to *Lydia's Funeral Video.*

I'm Lydia. Lydia Clark-Lin. Talking to you...

(to herself) **...to no one in particular, because I have to do this.**

> She looks back into the camera.

I'm here against my will.

I will explain what I just said.

Three nights ago, I have this dream. In the dream, I'm standing in this... desert, and then, from across a vast distance, I see this...bubble?...*thing* floating towards me.

> We hear the sound of three bubbles popping, ominously:
> *blop, blop, blop.*
>
> Lydia tenses at the sound.

And as it draws nearer and nearer, this strange suspended bubble, the earth shudders, the air crackles, and a voice says:

She is refusing, as usual, to accept responsibility.

A bubble appears, and she feels threatened.

What does a bubble signify? So fragile and insubstantial, yet so energized, buoyed up by its own lightness of being.

She can't relate.

Lydia raises her hand to act out the part of the Bubble now hovering before her. We hear the sound of a single bubble popping: *blop*.

Lydia speaks as BUBBLY, her fingers moving in sync with its words:

LYDIA, IT'S ME.

(suddenly suspicious) **And I say, "Who's 'me'? And how do you know my name?"**

(explaining, to the camera) **And then I realize what's going on. "This is a dream, Lydia, you're talking to yourself, of course you know your own name."**

And the bubble says:

Again, Lydia's fingers curl and uncurl in sync with Bubbly's words:

I AM THE EMBRYO GROWING INSIDE YOU.

I say, "Embryo? Isn't that, like, a fetus…thing?"

YES.

"Oh."

(relieved; it's been a misunderstanding) **"But I'm not pregnant."**

And it replies:

YES, YOU ARE.

And I think, "Oh god, if I'm pregnant, that means I slept with Manchild

Instead, she grumbles.   She resists.   She questions.

again, even though I promised Bernie I wouldn't, and she'll be pissed if she finds out."

And then I think, "Lydia, calm down. You're dreaming. You're not pregnant. This isn't real."

So I calm down. I breathe.

> She breathes.
> She notices something.

But then the bubble disturbs my calm breathing.

YOU *ARE* PREGNANT, it says. AND YOU WILL TERMINATE THIS PREGNANCY. BUT BEFORE YOU DO, YOU WILL MAKE A VIDEO. AND YOU WILL CALL IT, "LYDIA'S FUNERAL VIDEO."

(confused) "Funeral video?"

THE VIDEO THAT WILL BE SHOWN AT YOUR FUNERAL.

(nodding as if that totally makes sense) "Oh."

> She reflects a moment, then:

"But I'm not dying."

And the bubble says:

YES, YOU ARE.

And I think, "Oh my god, I *knew* I was sick! I was wondering if I had something, like a brain tumor, or stomach cancer, or some rare

She is perhaps prone to repeating the mistakes of her past, addicted to harmful behavior.

She knows this and experiences some feelings of remorse, but a part of her is proud of it, too; she relishes wallowing in the indisputable wrongness of her own actions.

degenerative disease that hasn't yet been discovered and therefore has no cure, or something like that. I *knew* I had *some*thing."

"...So, uh, which one is it?"

And the bubble says:

YOU HAVE FOUR WEEKS TO TERMINATE THIS PREGNANCY.
YOU HAVE FOUR WEEKS TO SHOOT "LYDIA'S FUNERAL VIDEO,"
THE VIDEO THAT WILL BE SHOWN AT YOUR FUNERAL.
FOUR WEEKS, STARTING...

NOW.

We hear the sound of a single bubble popping, with authority.

And I'm thinking, "I'm dreaming, I'm not dying in four weeks, and you're a figment of my idiot imagination."

And I've got a pen in my hand—one of those ultra-fine Sharpies that I love, I simply won't write with anything else—and I puncture the bubble. And as the bubble goes "pop," I wake up in bed.

She takes a quick look around, realizing: damnit.

And it's *Manchild*'s bed, and I'm thinking, "Oh no, I *did* sleep with him again. Lydia, he's getting married. To someone who's *not you*. Get out of this apartment right now and don't come back, okay? Easy. This is an easy thing to do that I am asking you to do. Because. It's perfectly logical. Go. Go now."

So I get dressed and leave his apartment, fantasizing that he'll be surprised, and a touch saddened, when he wakes up later and I'm not

And then, to have an anxiety justified and affirmed: the triumph of hearing she may have somewhat accurately predicted her own little portion of doom.

But of course, she grumbles.

She resists.

This is a woman who doesn't traffic in consequences. Consequences are for people with five-year plans, ten-year plans. She is not a woman with five-year plans or ten-year plans. She has no plans.

there. But knowing that he won't really care. Because that's just the kind of dynamic that Manchild and I share.

You know, *that* kind of dynamic: dysfunctional and prone to tragedy and chaos.

And that day I go to work at the bank as usual and engage myself in transactions involving money.

> She smiles, finding herself back in familiar territory.

That's what I'm meant to be engaged in—*destined* to be engaged in. Because you know, my name, Lydia—

> She cuts herself off, suddenly uncertain.

> Then, reasserting her authority of sorts:

Well maybe *you* don't know, but I spent a lot of time researching this subject growing up.

My mother claims to have selected my name "at random." I'd always tell her, "People don't select names at random. *Parents* don't select names at random for their *children*. You must have had a *reason* for naming me Lydia. I have to mean *some*thing."

And my mother would say, (imperious Condescending Mother voice) "Well why don't you ask your father? Maybe it's some ancient Chinese name, hmmm?"

Which is my mother's way of being *funny*, since I couldn't exactly "ask my father," seeing as he disappeared before I actually *exited* the womb. And even though the marriage has been kind of officially *over* for a few

She has no plans, yet still believes she is fated to be where she is.

Her job feels like a dead-end and destiny at the same time. Paradox. Ambiguity. Contradictions. "Life is so rich," she might think, as she pays a parking ticket online.

She has photographs of her father, but no memories of him; she grew up in his absence, an absence she knows he chose for himself.

decades now, we've still got this hyphenated last name, *Clark* hyphen *Lin*.

My mother thinks it sounds exotic and makes her stand out in her field, but I think she just has an unhealthy love-hate relationship with All Things Asian. The reason she "stands out" in her "field" is that her "field" is obsolete and her working in *television* as if it's still actually *relevant* anymore is an object of fascination in and of itself. Kind of like a curious little artifact of a bygone era.

> Lydia stops, hearing her mini-tirade in instant playback.

That was mean. Sorry.

I'm just a little, you know.

Stressed.

(a bit defensively) **Anyway, names *mean* something, right?**

Of course. They do.

> She smiles in anticipation: she has something fun to share, a secret of sorts.

And so what I discovered is that Lydia was actually this ancient country in western Anatolia, where Turkey is located today.

> As the lights shift, music evocative of Lydia's fantasy country of Lydia begins to play.

The name *Anatolia* itself is Turkish and means, "The Land Where the Sun Rises."

(explanatory aside) **It's from the Greek, *anatole*.**

But in her mother, someone who was always and aggressively there, she sees an Awful Uselessness that she fears might consume her, too.

Growing up, she foraged for meaning in the materials already available to her.

Raised in a bloodless, suburban landscape to which she never felt any real connection, she conjured up a fantasy country she could claim, a kingdom to call her own.

ACT ONE

(resuming narrative) **Lydia was a kingdom that ruled an area bordered by an abundance of water—four seas and a river: the Black Sea to the north; the inner sea, Propontis, or the Marmara Sea, to the northwest; the Aegean to the west; the Mediterranean—the Lycian Coast specifically—to the south; and the River Halys, to the east.**

(explanatory aside) **I didn't know where any of those places were, either, because I'm, you know, an American. But I googled it. Fascinating.**

(resuming narrative) **Lydia is also home to the highest peak in the land, Mount Ararat—sixteen thousand feet high, a volcano—said to be the final resting place of Noah's Ark after the Great Flood described in the Book of Genesis of the Old Testament.**

(explanatory aside) **I'm not really a religious person, but I thought that whole Ark of the Covenant thing was an important detail, and it would be criminal to leave it out.**

(resuming narrative) **The Lydian Era was brief, but brilliant. Lydia ruled for a period of a hundred and fifty years in the seventh and sixth centuries B.C.**

During that time, it became the first country to *mint coins* and create *official currency*—the oldest coins ever discovered are Lydian coins dating back to 650 B.C., and the kingdom was known for its fabulous riches. The name of the last king of Lydia, Croesus, is synonymous with wealth. And there was a river that flowed through the country of Lydia that was said to carry *glittering bits of gold* in its sediment.

Lydia has, in her mind's eye, conjured up this particular feature of the landscape; she gazes at it now, mesmerized.

She fetishes her would-be Turkish roots, imagining herself heir to something exotic, magical, fulfilling—a child of the rising sun.	She loves pronouncing the names, as if she is working a spell: *Propontis. Marmara. Aegean. Lycian. River Halys.*	*Ararat.*		*Lyd. Ee. En.*

Lydia. *That* is the story of my name. Its history, its legacy, its destiny. My inheritance!

> She luxuriates in her Lydian fantasy a moment longer as the music reaches its climax.
>
> Then the music abruptly cuts out, and the usual lights are restored.
>
> Regaining awareness of the camera, she continues in a more restrained manner.

So I figured getting a job at Chase was a good way to get started with that.

(pre-emptively defending herself against judgement) **It's not about greed or lust for money or anything. It's more that I feel I should be *involved* with currency, with monetary units. Involved in a tactile, day-to-day way.**

> Hrmm...a wrinkle occurs to her.

Although I've been working there about five years now and I don't exactly feel like I'm *fulfilling my destiny.*

I mean, I do feel tolerably useful when I guide a person through the often intimidating process of opening his or her first money market account, but...

It's just not the same thing. Not the same thing as *destiny fulfillment.*

I guess I'm just not doing it right yet.

Anyway.

I go to work at the bank as usual, but I'm not feeling *as usual.* I can't

There is so little in her life over which she commands knowledge, so she revels in the small puddles of information she does possess.

Still, she prefers methods of realizing one's potential that are not labor-intensive; eventually, her destiny and inheritance will make themselves manifest all on their own.

focus on anything, I keep hearing the bubble music playing over and over in my head, and there's this *tugging* at the bottom of my stomach. It's almost like I'm back in high school and doing things like theater and untreated clinical depression.

So I leave work a few minutes early, telling my supervisor I am feeling sick, and I stop off at a Walgreens on my way home to buy a pregnancy test. You know, just in case.

Not that I believe my dream was some sort of *prophetic dream* or anything, but you know. Just in case.

Of course I'm nervous, and when the pharmacist asks to see my I.D., I freeze up—I completely forgot that now you have to be twenty-one or over to get a test—and ever since I turned eighteen over a decade ago I've always had this *little problem* of looking like a fifteen-year-old—and the pharmacist is giving me suspicious looks, because everyone's so *weird* about pregnancy these days.

I mean I want to tell her, "Relax! It's not like I'm gonna try and abort it right in front of you, alright? I can go to Canada for that. Besides, I've still got three weeks before it's illegal, so you can stop *looking* at me that way."

> Oops: Lydia's sort of exploded at the innocent pharmacist who's just doing her job.
>
> Lydia continues, somewhat sheepishly:

And the pharmacist is explaining how this test works by checking for a hormone in the saliva or something, and she instructs me to listen for the three consecutive beeps before checking the color of the light—red for not pregnant, green for pregnant.

Routines can be helpful.

She dismisses the still oozing wounds of her youth with a rhetorical shrug-off, as if she would close them up in denying their existence.

She has other things to focus on, she tells herself.

(imitating the super-cheerful tone of the pharmacist) "You know, if you're pregnant, green for go!" the pharmacist says—which I think they're supposed to say to make pregnancy sound like happy fun time and encourage you to go ahead and have the kid—Bernie's told me all about this stuff.

And I tell her, "Thanks! I'll explain all that to my friend, (searching for a name) Lllli...zabeth. Because this isn't even for me, you know. I'm just helping. A friend."

I don't know why, I just felt I should tell her that.

So when I get home, I wake up my computer to calm down, I watch some Comedy Central for a while, and I'm a little too sleepy to take that test. And I drift off.

And as soon as I hit unconsciousness...

> We hear a sweet and mysterious sort of lullaby: Bubbly's music.
>
> The lights change as Lydia enters the dream.

...there I am in that desert again, with this bubble floating towards me across a vast distance.

(conceding, as she sees it) Although the distance seems less vast, somehow.

> Her hand rises again, to assume the role of Bubbly.

And I'm thinking, "Oh no, not *you* again."

And Bubbly says:

ᒪᑫ ᐤ ᒡ ᑫ ᐤᐤᐤᐤᒡ ᑲᐤᑦᐤ ᑲᐧᐤᐤᑫᑫᐧᑫ ᐤᐧ ᐤᑲᐧᐧᐤᑫ ᑫᐤᑫᐧᐤ ᐤᐤᑫ ᐤᐤᑫᑫᐧᐤ

Important, pressing, here and now things.	For instance, sleep.		Sleep, with a few complications.

ACT ONE

YOU HAVEN'T STARTED SHOOTING "LYDIA'S FUNERAL VIDEO."
IT'S TIME TO BEGIN.

And I say, "I told you, *I'm not dying*. And even if I *were* dying, I don't know anything about making a video. If you're so *obsessed* with this idea of the video, go invade my mother's dreams instead—she's the one who talks to cameras all the time. I bet she'd *love* to make my funeral video."

YOU MUST MAKE "LYDIA'S FUNERAL VIDEO."

"Leave me alone," I say, and I try to go back to sleep.

Except I *am* asleep, and I can't seem to get out of that desert, with Bubbly *staring* at me.

> She watches it staring at her.

(acknowledging) Well, it's a bubble, so it's not really *staring*, but...you know.

You know how bubbles can kind of *look* like they're *staring* at you?

> Suddenly, she sees something.

And then something happens.

The bubble starts to get cinched in around its center, like someone's tightening an invisible little belt around it, and Bubbly starts to look more like a peach—I love peaches!—and the cleavage gets deeper and deeper and then the thing just...splits...

> Her other hand rises to join the first:

...Into two separate bubbles attached to one another. And it looks at me

Even in sleep, she doesn't miss an opportunity, however out of the way, to casually slander her mother.	Not that Lydia would actually suggest her mother would welcome the death of her own daughter; that would be so extreme.	Still, Lydia has her illustrative anecdotes. For instance, when Lydia was a child in Halifax, there was a favorite peach tree growing in the yard behind the house, but her mother had it cut down.	Probably, Lydia believes, because it was something that pleased Lydia, and her mother felt strongly that losing things one cares about builds character.

and says:

<u>DO IT. MAKE "LYDIA'S FUNERAL VIDEO."</u>

And then it divides a*gain*, both of them do...

> Lydia's hands fall away from their representation of Bubbly, and Bubbly is, well, out of her hands:

...So now it's *four* bubbles speaking to me in this one bubbly voice, and I say, "No, I can't. I have to work, and I have a destiny—I think I do, anyway—and I don't have the time right now to go crazy, so please leave me alone."

And bubbly-mass divides a*gain*, so now it's *eight* bubbles speaking to me in this one bubbly voice, which resounds across the desert as it says:

(big resounding voice in cute bubbly voice way) "No."

(suddenly indignant) And I can't be*lieve* this self-proclaimed *embryo thing* is actually trying to *intimidate* me by getting bigger. What, like might makes right?

And I've got that pen in my hand again, and pop-pop-pop-pop-pop-pop-pop-*pop*, I pop them all out of existence, and I go into a different dream.

> Bubbly's musical theme ends abruptly, and Lydia is back in her living room.

But the next day, I am experiencing...some problems.

That tug in my stomach is even worse, I'm hearing the bubble music in my head, and I'm having flashbacks to junior high and playing a tree

Lydia would like to believe her schedule is packed, her day crammed with high priority tasks and responsibilities; she needs to believe she is necessary to the world in some way.

These bubbles with their bizarre demands threaten the comfortable narrative she has constructed for herself. She moves instinctively to eradicate this threat with a few quick jabs of the pen: a rare instance of taking decisive action.

in the school production of *Lord of the Rings*, adapted for the stage—it seemed like a radical idea at the time. And I stumble in my speech several times while talking to clients, and my supervisor John is giving me funny looks, and my sweet peppy co-worker Kimmie keeps asking me *really cheerfully* if I'd like an Advil or a glass of water, and everyone's wondering, "What's wrong with Lydia? What's wrong with Lydia?" because there's *clearly* something *wrong* with Lydia.

And I realize I didn't brush my hair or put on my make-up before leaving my apartment, *and* I haven't updated my Facespace status since that morning, which is *kind* of like a nonverbal way of saying, "Lock me up, I'm crazy!"

Maybe the apocalypse will come tomorrow.

I make it through the day somehow and I get home, and I see that test lying on the table, but I still don't take it.

I wake up my computer, watch some more streaming video, and at some point I fall asleep...

> Bubbly theme music and dream lights return; Lydia is dismayed.

And there's Bubbly, right away...

> A tangle of small spherical blue lights suspended from the ceiling glows softly as BUBBLY comes into more physical being.

...And Bubbly is many bubbles, so many bubbles I can't count them, and it drifts over to me and says:

> The blue lights glow in sync with Bubbly's speech.

These memories might belong to someone else, they are so far away, and so saturated with a color that doesn't exist in her daily palette.

So she returns to her habitual remedy for feeling unsettled or destabilized: ceding all brain activity to the authorship of others.

"I don't want to make a video...I don't even know *how*."

YOU HAVE A VIDEO CAMERA, JUST TURN IT ON.
YOU HAVE TO MAKE "LYDIA'S FUNERAL VIDEO."

"But I'm not dying.

"I mean, I don't *really* think I'm dying.

She stops, suddenly uncertain.

"Am I?"

YOU *ARE* DYING.

This sinks in; a moment.

And part of me, somehow, *relaxes,* when I hear that. I don't even want to question it anymore. Like, "It's okay, I'm dying. I won't have to worry soon."

But I'm not sure.

(back to Bubbly) "*You*'re not even real. I may not even *be* pregnant."

YOU *ARE* PREGNANT.

YOU *ARE* DYING.
YOU HAVE TWENTY-SIX DAYS REMAINING TO SHOOT "LYDIA'S FUNERAL VIDEO."

(as if confirming the terms of a deal) "So, you're not going to leave me alone unless I do this, right?"

A strategy which can work for only so long.

And Bubbly nods, the way an enormous mass of undifferentiated bubbles nods.

If you haven't seen it before, it is *very* impressive—you just don't argue with an enormous mass of undifferentiated bubbles. It would be... unwise.

"Okay, you win. Fine. You win, Bubbly!"

> Bubbly's musical theme cuts out, the blue lights vanish, and Lydia is back in her apartment.

And I'm awake.

And I take the test.

And the green light goes on: green for go.

(calmly freaking out) **And I call in to work and tell them I am having emergency health issues and will be taking all of my sick days for the year.**

And they remind me that if I take the full five days I'll have exhausted my annual healthcare allowance and won't be covered again until July first, which of course I knew—I mean, I'm lucky my employer offers me health insurance options at *all*—not that I've even seen a doctor *once* in the last few years because the co-pay is so high, which is probably why no one's diagnosed me with whatever I'm dying of yet. But...

...But maybe the apocalypse will come tomorrow.

> She gradually returns to full awareness of the video camera, and the task at hand.

So.

Does she want to be assured that it is not her choice, and that she must simply obey?

Could she be free from responsibility? The possibility shimmers before her, tantalizing and seductive.

That was a few hours before I started filming this.

I had to go out and get some more memory cards for my camera because all the cards I had were full from some stupid stuff I'd recorded earlier—just me messing around while procrastinating on my work with monetary units—procrastination can really eat up a person's memory...

> She trails off.
>
> Suddenly, she has an idea.

I'll ask Bernie about it.

That's my friend, Dr. Bernadette Tayag.

(proudly) Yes, *the* Doctor Bernadette Tayag—aka the Bay Area's Death Angel.

(realizing) She's not going to be too thrilled about all this, actually...

...But I think she can help...lend some, uh, *credibility*...to the proceedings.

> She begins to gather her things—keys, bag, coat.

...*If* I can get her away from her work long enough.

Bernie really needs a break from all those crazy protesters in Halifax. I mean, you try to do something good, and *look* where it gets you.

> She turns to go.

She is so accustomed to dismissing the significance of so many aspects of her life that the dismissal itself has become a reflex.

What is the nature of our procrastination? What do we do when we are avoiding something else? Can we track it?

Can we be so certain that such hours are misspent, that the unintended yield of this time is without value?

SCENE 2

Lydia's apartment.
Later that night.

BERNIE turns to the audience. Suited up in a military-style jacket, Bernie moves decisively; her attitude is direct and no-nonsense.

Fuck, Lydia.

So first of all, you know that I'm a doctor whose primary focus at the present time is providing *abortion services*, right?

But you're telling me that your developing *four-day-old embryo* is *talking* to you, in a very human and conscious way, right?

But there are some people who never have to worry about whether their hours, any number of them, have been misspent. Some people never have to wonder if the yield of their time, intended or otherwise, is of value.

Their hours lived have been lived with a purpose so clear, a drive so relentless, that the value is never in question. Their lives soar like arrows in perfect flight, released by the sure hand of an experienced archer, moving with confidence toward their targets.

They do not waver from their paths. They do not agonize over choices.

Probably, they do not sleep with the fiancés of other people.

So, *that* part's not cool with me. I am *not* down with this whole "my embryo is conscious and alive" bullshit. *No.* That is hella wrong. This is typical *crazy Lydia* imagination.

Second, a funeral video? What funeral, Lydia? Since when are you dying?

You think you're dying not because you've experienced any *actual symptoms* that might indicate that you have a fatal condition, but because your crazy imagination sent you a crazy dream?

Lydia, you may be my girl and I may love you, but you have *never* had any prophetic dreams, alright? It's just not your thing.

Now I can make sure we get you a physical later and run some standard tests just to be sure, but if you're relying on a *dream* as your primary source of evidence here—I'm going with the *Lydia's-motherfucking-crazy* theory.

Third: What the fuck, you're pregnant? When the fuck did *that* happen? And how, when your best friend has been throwing free contraceptives at you for years?

And not just *any* free contraceptives, Lydia, I've been giving you the *good* shit—all the beta versions of the hottest new high-tech condoms out on the market. The heated ones, the vibrating ribbed ones—there was even that freaky shape-shifting one—the smart condom? With the chip and the memory latex?

What the fuck else do you *want* from me, Lydia? You are an *adult*, you need me to hold your hand for you while you practice safe sex? You need me to accompany you on your *dates*—or whatever the fuck they are—and put the condoms on *for* you? *Fuck.*

Lydia experiences a small emotional pleasure spike at Bernie's suggestion that she has an imagination.

A part of her always quietly worries that she has none.

She wishes she could access the impressive rage that Bernie seems to engage so effortlessly; Lydia feels limp and emotionally flat next to her spirited friend.

And who'd you get pregnant *with*, by the way?

Because it better not have happened with mister *Manchild* who's about to *get married*—you know, the one you *promised* me you wouldn't see again? If you're pregnant, it *better* have been some kind of immaculate conception or some new guy I've never heard about, or I will be *hella pissed*!

Forget that, I *am* hella pissed—damnit you crazy halfbreed, you are upsetting me and forcing me to be unpro*fess*ional.

> Bernie takes a moment.

Hold up, hold up.

I am now channeling Doctor Tayag so I can give you my professional *doctor* advice.

> Sitting down, she collects herself, focusing on her breathing.

Channeling the professional inside me, channeling the *professional* inside me—

—Shut *up*, Lydia, you *better* let me channel if you don't want me to execute you my*self*.

> She breathes a moment.

Okay.

(calmly, as if to a child) So, Lydia, you think you're pregnant?

Well don't worry, we're gonna talk about this to*gether*, and we're gonna work out a *plan*. No one's judging you.

She feels comforted; whenever Bernie refers to her as a mongrel, the friendship is re-affirmed.	Does Lydia feel a twinge of jealousy at Bernie's effortless performance of expertise? Bernie is a real adult, with a profession, a title, a useful skill set...	...Lydia has little more than an ability to navigate Chase's complicated and proprietary database software.

Now, if you're pregnant, you know you have a couple of options. You can choose to let the pregnancy continue, or you can choose to terminate the pregnancy. Now I wish I could tell you to take all the time you need to consider those options, but you know the reality.

So. Lydia. Do you know what you want to do?

Okay.

So you know the law requires that a woman seeking an abortion complete the termination treatment within twenty-eight days of conception—after that, I can't help you. I'm being watched really closely right now, and I need to make sure that all my units are operating legally, so please don't wait, Lydia.

I can get you a sonogram later to see how far along you are, *if* you're along at all—those at-home pregnancy tests aren't a hundred percent accurate anyway, especially within the first few days.

And if you *are* pregnant, hopefully your crazy dream is actually right about this happening only a few days ago. Which is *not to say* that I think you have prophetic dreams, you *don't*.

But if that embryo has been developing for more than twenty-six days, well...you're fucked. You're having a child, anyway.

(almost under her breath, but not quite) **And lord knows that child will be hella fucked up...**

28

Bernie had demonstrated an ambitious and decisive nature from an early age.

Lydia often imagined that if she hung close enough, she might absorb some of that unwavering confidence, soak it up like a sponge.

...Well, not *hell*a fucked up, Lydia. But, come on: a little bit fucked up, right?

> Bernie laughs.

But Lydia, you *haven't* seen him again though, right? Mister Manchild?

> She laughs again.
>
> She looks at Lydia.
>
> She stops laughing.

...Right?

(realizing)...Oh, no. No *way*! I am so *pissed* at you Lydia!

Turn off the motherfucking camera!

> Bernie storms off.

Yeah, right.

SCENE 3

The news desk at Greater Halifax News.
Day 4.

We hear the *Greater Halifax News* music as CYNTHIA CLARK-LIN prepares—checking out her reflection, positioning a loose strand of hair, smoothing her collar. At the music's conclusion, the lights come up fully on Cynthia, expertly coiffed and all smiles, as she turns to deliver her report.

And it looks like San Francisco-based doctor Bernadette Tayag has won another victory. Known as the Bay Area's "Death Angel," Doctor Tayag is the founder and director of Family Planning Mobile Services, or FPMS, a business offering abortion services via a fleet of former military armored vehicles repurposed as mobile clinics. The popular FPMS was launched in the wake of the Colorado v. Planned Parenthood Supreme Court decision, which found that the not-for-profit healthcare provider had been violating the human rights of fertilized eggs for decades.

This morning, Doctor Tayag announced that her FPMS fleet will be expanding by a dozen new units. Previously operating only in San Francisco neighborhoods, FPMS will now deploy its mobile clinics to Richmond, Halifax, Oakland, San Mateo, San Jose, and East Palo Alto.

The expansion of Doctor Tayag's Family Planning Mobile Services comes just weeks after the killing of an abortion doctor shut down Florida's only remaining clinic, a private practice based in Miami.

Here in Halifax, California, residents opposing the introduction of FPMS units in the area have vowed to offer resistance.

Until next time, this is Cynthia Clark-Lin, reporting with *Greater Halifax News* at six.

> The *Greater Halifax News* musical outro plays, and lights go out on Cynthia.

SCENE 4

Lydia's apartment again.
Day 5.

A relatively contrite BERNIE has returned, wishing to reconcile.

Alright. So I apologize for losing my temper earlier.

I am now ready to help my good friend, Lydia, make this creepy-ass video.

She moves her way over to the couch, positioning herself in relation to the camera.

So you want me to talk about you, right? Like a testimonial?

There is probably so little to say.

She chuckles.

She settles in to address the camera.

So. A little Bernie-Lydia backstory...

Well, we both grew up in Halifax—(to Lydia) as if that's not trauma enough, right?—(back to camera) and we met in Lydia's backyard when I was eight.

She smiles at the discovery of the memory, then at the memory itself.

I'd been playing operation on my dolls all day, and I realized that for my next procedure—a heart transplant on this ballerina—I needed to collect a few more key pieces of equipment.

Like a heart with which to replace the existing, failing heart—which was failing because she had to do ballet all the time instead of just kickin' it with her homegirls and having a *real* childhood.

I'd already released my other patients—whom I'd healed, of course, of all their illnesses—and I thought it would constitute cruel and *unusual* punishment to ask one of my newly recovered patients to return to my little clinic just so I could remove his heart to help out this ballerina chick.

So I decide to go for a little walk to see if I can't find someone who doesn't need their heart.

And I turn the corner, and I hear this voice talking *very clearly* about money, and minted coins, and rivers flowing with gold.

And I get closer, and I look into the backyard of this house, and there's

But childhood is always a reliably promising subject. Childhood has a certain glow around it; everything and everyone can be charming, because they haven't yet had the time to be proven otherwise.

An activity that is disturbing and sad becomes sweet and endearing when viewed through the lens of childhood.

One of Lydia's only sources of entertainment, pre-best friend: delivering speeches about her name to a rapt, immobile, and captive audience.

this little Asian girl about my age, talking to a bunch of stuffed animals about the name *Lydia*.

She's like a little motherfuckin' professor this girl, going off about five hundred B.C. this, and western Turkey that, and I'm like, "What the fuck?" Another little Asian kid—(to Lydia) probably the only other one in Halifax, right? And of course we're both busy being industrious and doing shit, all alone, no friends...

(to the camera again) **And I watch her for a while, and I wonder...**

      Bernie scans the assembly of stuffed animals, searching... Ah, there's one.

...if that teddy bear...

(finding her target)...or maybe that *big stuffed rabbit* might not be ready to kick the bucket.

So I go up to this girl in the middle of her lecture, and I tell her I am very sorry to interrupt, but I need to get a heart to one of my patients.

And she says, "You need a heart?"

And I say, "Yes, one of my patients needs a transplant, or she'll die."

And this girl says, "Oh, well you can have mine if you want."

And I say, "I can have your heart?"

And she says, "Yeah sure, I just need it back later. You have to have all your organs intact for the apocalypse or you won't be saved."

There were none among her inanimate, stuffed listeners to ignore or to mock her, as was so often the case in the company of her mother or classmates.

But this new girl did not mock; she was too busy keeping her priorities intact.

The closest Lydia got to having priorities was an early fascination with the End of Days. Even as a child, she was mesmerized by the idea of a final reckoning--a time that would end it all.

See, *clearly* this girl does not have an under*stand*ing of how a heart transplant *works*.

And I say, "Girl, if you give your heart away for a heart transplant, god may bless you for your generosity, but you are *not* getting that heart back."

And my girl says—(to Lydia) 'cause you were already my girl, at that point—(to camera) my girl says, "Oh, I guess I should keep it then. Maybe you can have one of *their* hearts, instead?"

Right? And she's pointing at the poor little bunny rabbits and teddy bears who can't defend themselves—reading my *mind*.

And we agree that the rabbit will work *perfectly*—since it's a little-known medical fact that rabbit hearts and ballerina hearts are compatible—and Lydia asks if she can see the operation, and I say, "Sure." And we return to my operating table, which is a picnic table. And I begin the operation.

And Lydia says, "You're not doing it right."

And I say, "How the fuck would *you* know? Are you some kind of *doctor*?"

And Lydia says, "Because if you were doing it right, there'd be blood. And I don't see any blood."

So I had to *explain* to her, "Well of course there's *blood*, Lydia, but it's the *invisible* kind? You know?"

And she says she didn't know. And then she asks me, "Well, how do you know anything's happening if you can't see it?"

 And I tell her:

Informed that giving her heart away would constitute a more final sacrifice than she had in mind, Lydia withdraws the offer.

Uninspiring as it was, Lydia had always tended to refrain from sacrifice and battle; she was, she felt, more naturally inclined toward cowardice.

For this, she might blame socialization, and then grudgingly acknowledge the overwhelming number of exceptions to the rule. And then grudgingly acknowledge that exceptions can invalidate or redefine the rule. And then feel lame for a while.

The decidedly un-gory nature of the medical intervention was disappointing; some part of her craved a bloody, desperate, high-stakes landscape.

"You just have to feel these things out. Trust me: it's a doctor thing."

And she was impressed with my medical expertise—(to Lydia) as well she should have been—(back to camera) and after the operation she asked if I wanted to hear about her name, and if I wanted to be in one of her plays.

And that's how I met this girl. Our friendship is founded on a sacrificial stuffed animal heart and invisible blood. And just general weirdness.

> Bernie notices the general weirdness.

Like this. This video...this is *very weird*, too, Lydia.

Actually, I think this may well be the weirdest thing you've done...

(remembering)...Since that basement ghost dragon thing! The one where you had me playing the stupid widow who was like, "Oh, I wonder why the door to the basement is open, when no one's been down to that room for twenty-odd years? Well, even though I'm *all alone*, and *completely defenseless*, I think I'll go down and investigate anyway, because what the fuck, maybe I can learn something about the basement."

> Bernie laughs.

I am *not* making that shit up, I remember that one! It was *called*, "Psychotic Ghost in the Basement," by Lydia Clark-Lin. Damn, Lydia, I remember your work better than *you* do. We put it up in the yard at Halifax—that was when the neighborhood kids started calling us the two Chink Chicks—remember that shit?

Your mom was *bella* pissed! "They are *not* chinks. *I'm* her mother—Lydia is half-white. And Bernadette here is practically *Spanish*!"

In spite of her protests, Lydia is proud that Bernie is referencing something she wrote when she was younger.	At the same time (because any one moment is so exquisitely complex), Lydia experiences a sharp pang at the reference.	It has been so long, Lydia thinks, since she wrote anything at all.

I was like, *"Pinay,* bitch, I am *not* Spanish! Fuck that."

Bernie laughs, then notices the time.

Shit, Lydia, I gotta head over to Halifax.

She starts gathering her things to leave, continuing to talk to Lydia.

We didn't finish installing the new unit yesterday because some dumb shit damaged an oxygen tank—small town vigilantes, all angry and impotent.

They're like little tiny lapdogs—toothpick legs all trembly, hearts beating a hundred times a second, yap-yap-yapping at you like they think they're actually scary? You know, not really dangerous, but annoying as shit?

So who else are you gonna put on this video?

Oh, what about that hyper-cheerful girl from work you always talk about? What's her name? Muffy or Winky or something? Titty?

Kimmie, right. You should talk to Kimmie.

Bernie smiles, and slides into her jacket.

They remember the
desolate strangeness of
Halifax:

They felt themselves to
be the only two people
there with a heartbeat.

SCENE 5

A restaurant in San Francisco.
Afternoon, Day 6.

KIMMIE spots Lydia and waves excitedly. Brimming with enthusiasm and wrapped in a poofy pink scarf, she takes a seat opposite the camera.

Hiiiii Lydia! So you're doing like a little film about your life? What a super-fun *project*!

And I *totally* feel like we're some kind of *crazy* undercover agents or something, meeting like this when everyone thinks you're *home sick*!

I mean, when John asked me, "Kimmie, where are you going?" I told him, "Oh," I said, "I'm just going to meet a friend. For *lunch*."

While Lydia feels herself to be in many ways above Kimmie, she will concede that Kimmie embodies freshness, lightness, immediacy; her enthusiasm is irrepressible.

And, to Lydia, a bit grating.

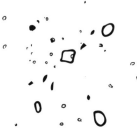

She gives a conspiratorial wink, pleased with herself.

And he was all, "Well we didn't go to the expense of getting our own kitchen and food services staff just so *you* could go off-site for lunch all the time!" You know, all grumpy and angry, the way John always is?

She laughs a tee-hee-hee sort of giggle.

And I *told* him, I said, "*John*, this is the *first* time I've done it *all fiscal year*!" Which was totally totally *true*!

But you know, I wasn't telling him the *full* truth, because I didn't tell him I was meeting *you*.

So I feel like we're doing these *secretive* things, or like we're on some super-exciting *adventure*! Doesn't it kind of feel that way?

(a bit disappointed) **No?** It doesn't feel that way?

(remembering) **Oh!** So are you going to be coming back to work? I think it's sooo, so-so-so *crazy*! That you got *sick* like that with *no warning*. Shouldn't you give a lot more notice when you get really sick like that, so people can prepare for it?

(sympathetic) **I** guess sometimes you can't really see it coming, can you, when you get really, really-really sick, huh?

(inspecting Lydia) **You** *look* fine...you *seem* fine.

You *know*, (looking closer) you actually look *better*, like you've got this healthy *glow* or something! Did you just get some kind of *spa* treatment

ꙮ◠◗◠◦◦◦◗◠◦◦◗◦ ◗ ◠ ◗ ◠ ◗ ◠ ◠ ◗◠◦◦◗ ◠◗◦◦◗◦◠◦◦◦◦◦◠◦◦◦ ◦◦◦ ◦ ◦◦◦◗◠◠◦◗◠◗◦◦◠◦◦◦◦◦◠◦◦◠ ◗◯◉◦◦◗◠◠◦◦◦◗◠◗◦◦◦◦◦◗◠◗

Lydia thinks, privately, that she does a better John imitation.

She begins to question the wisdom of interviewing this cheerful woman for her project; such energy might compromise the gravitas required of a funeral video.

Is Kimmie mocking her, Lydia wonders? Does she know?

or something?

You *didn't*?

Oh! You want me to talk to the *camera*. Okay!

(adjusting herself) So, I'm talking *to the camera*, and I'm talking about...*Lydia*!

> Kimmie stares a moment, smiling.
>
> She seems to draw a blank.
>
> She looks to Lydia for help.

What should I say?

> Kimmie looks uncertain.

Okay...

...Well, she can always make me *laugh!!!*

> She laughs.

And she seems to be really, um... (suddenly serious, nodding gravely) *diligent*...at her job at *Chase*.

> Kimmie is at a loss again.

What else should I say?

> Kimmie listens a moment.

Okay...

Lydia can't tell; Kimmie seems too dense to be that perceptive.

But then again, Lydia is a judgmental person, prone to making gross misjudgments, of character and circumstance.

Lydia is mildly offended that her colleague should need prompting to talk about her.

ACT ONE ...So I've known Lydia for a few years now—(to Lydia) What is it, two, three...

(incredulous) *Four*? (laughing it off) Who can tell, the years all run into one another don't they? In *twenty* years we'll be saying the *same thing*. "How long have we been working together? Ten, eleven, *twenty* years?"

> She laughs.
>
> Kimmie continues, oblivious and on a roll.

Oh! But maybe we won't live that long, because the *world will end*!!! (finding this hilarious) You're so *funny*, Lydia, so *obsessed* with the (struggling with the word) acapa—acapa—

—(nodding) Um-hmm, apocalypse!

> Kimmie keeps nodding and smiling a moment, staring at the camera.

So what else should I say?

> Kimmie listens a moment.
>
> Her brightness dims considerably.
>
> Then, she attempts to take Lydia's suggestion.

Well, it's a *job*, right... (going into an autopilot worker-drone voice) We enter account information into the computer, we process transfer and withdrawal requests, we open accounts for new clients—

(snapping back to her usual voice, finding the humor)—It's really not that hard, *anyone* can do it.

> Kimmie sees Lydia's expression.

ꙮꙮꙮ꙳ꙮ꙳ꙮꙮ꙳ꙮꙮꙮꙮꙮꙮꙮꙮꙮꙮꙮꙮꙮꙮ꙳ꙮꙮꙮꙮꙮꙮꙮꙮꙮ꙳ꙮ꙳ꙮꙮꙮꙮ꙳ꙮꙮ꙳ꙮꙮꙮꙮꙮꙮꙮꙮꙮ꙳ꙮꙮꙮꙮ

This isn't really all that hilarious to Lydia.

She still cherishes the idea of being—in any remote, quiet way— exceptional.

Oh I didn't mean it like *that*! But it's a *job*, Lydia, you know that! It's a *job*, that you *do*. So you can do the things you actually *like* doing in life.

Oh, are we done already?

Even if all evidence
indicates otherwise.

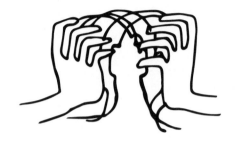

SCENE 6

Lydia's apartment.
Evening, Day 7.

LYDIA is alone, her head in her hands; she seems defeated and exhausted.

She looks up and acknowledges the camera, resenting it, but surrendered to the mission.

Phantom pregnancy, day seven.

Well, as it turns out, I actually *am* pregnant, and according to the sonogram Bernie gave me, seven *days* pregnant—I guess the little fucker was right after all—but I still think of it as a *phantom pregnancy*, seeing as I am still visited in my dreams by a phantom of sorts, who tells me I'm dying and gives me instructions...

There is, however, some consolation in imagining she has an otherworldly companion, even one who is vaguely threatening, in a bizarrely cute sort of way.

At least and at last, it seems, she has finally joined the ranks of those whose lives are punctuated by encounters with the unknown.

Clearly, Lydia is feeling some hostility here.

So last night, I'm just lying in bed, rolling this plastic bottle of pills around in my hands—the pills Bernie gave me.

(reciting the instructions) I'm supposed to take two—with water and food—and then, twenty-four hours later, take the other two, with water and food. And then it will be, you know, done. And stuff.

I'm rolling the bottle back and forth in my hands, and somehow...

Bubbly's theme music and the dream lights return.

...I'm in the desert again.

And there's Bubbly...

A blue tangle of bubbly lights materialize, glowing softly.

...a shape-shifting tower of tiny bubbles, billowing before me, and sparkling.

And I say,

(suddenly really seeing Bubbly; meaning it) "Wow, you're beautiful."

And Bubbly says:

YOU'RE THE ONE IMAGINING ME.

And I say, (confused, now) "But I thought you were real."

She enjoys the officialness of having an official prescription with official instructions to be followed. Explicit directives suggesting a sense of responsibility, however cheaply earned, fortify her.

Has some part of her come to crave this desert? This blank expanse wants nothing from her, and expects nothing.

And Bubbly says:

I AM REAL. AND YOU HAVE TWENTY-ONE DAYS LEFT TO SHOOT 'LYDIA'S FUNERAL VIDEO' AND TERMINATE THIS PREGNANCY.

And I say, (indignant) "Yes, I believe I can do the math. People who work with monetary units *do* have a basic grasp of arithmetic, thanks."

(ignoring Lydia) IN ORDER TO COMPLETE THE VIDEO, YOU MUST PERFORM THREE TASKS.

"That sounds like...a *lot* of tasks."

THE FIRST TASK IS TO INTERVIEW CYNTHIA CLARK-LIN.

"That would be my mother. And *that* would *not* go over well—the two of us don't really...get along."

THE SECOND TASK IS TO INTERVIEW GIN.

"That would be Manchild—*also* not a good idea. He's got better things to do than talk to me. Like send out wedding invitations, for example."

THE THIRD TASK IS TO DO THREE SETS OF STANDUP COMEDY AT AN OPEN MIC.

A beat. Lydia stares.

(incredulous) "Standup *comedy*? At an *open mic*?? What the hell does that have to do with anything?"

YOU GO TO THAT CAFÉ REGULARLY TO WATCH.
YOU HAVE ALWAYS WANTED TO TRY.

No one's supposed to know about that—I keep forgetting Bubbly has this

And yet, there is something so easy, a cleanness and a clarity, about A Task.

A Task resists the terrific grayness of ambiguity. At the mention of "three tasks," she envisions an orderly, check-boxed list, awaiting completion. How specific, how do-able!

At the mention of the café, something thrills.

whole...*omniscient* thing going on.

> She breaks more fully from the dream encounter with Bubbly, and turns
> to the camera to confess:

Well, see...so there's this *thing*.

Thursday nights, they have these standup comedy open mics at this
laundromat/coffee shop hybrid establishment by my apartment.

> Lydia relaxes into this subject, as the lights change and we hear the
> sound of soft chatter and espresso machines in the background.

I've been going there for years, by myself.

(reassuring) Just to watch. I've never told anyone about it. You know,
except for Bernie, of course. And Gin.

It's kind of like a guilty pleasure, I guess. (a bit giddy, reliving it) Watching
people getting up there on stage...humiliating themselves. It can be
very...cathartic.

Usually I'm there a few hours, until, once again, I'm one of two people
who's actually stuck around until the bitter end—the other person being
the host—

> She cuts herself off, bringing herself back to the present moment with
> the camera.

But no one's supposed to know that. It's, you know, a *private* thing.

> Finished with her explanation, she returns to the dream encounter with
> Bubbly, picking up where she left off.

"For your information, I go to 'that café' because 'that café' is also a

ᒐ·ᐤ ᐤ ᒐ ᒐ Ꝺᐤⸯᐤ ᐤ ᑕ ᔓᐤᔡᔡᐤ Ꝺᐤᔡᔡ ᐤ Ꝺᐤᐤ·ᐤᐤ.ᐤ.ᐤᑕᔡᐤᐤᐤ ᐤᐤᐟ ᔡ ᔡᐤᑊᐤᐤ ᐤ ᔡ ᐤ Ꝺ ᐤ ᐤᔡᐤᑕᐤᐤᐤ Ꝺᔡᐤᔡᐤᐤ ᐤ Ꝺᔡᐤᔡ ᐤ ᔡᐤ ᐤ ᔡ·ᐤᔡᔡᐟ ᐤ ᔡᐤᐤᔡ ᐤᐤ ᐤᐤ ᐤ ᐟᐟ ᐤᐤᔡ ᐤᔡ

A frisson of excitement,
or dread.

But, thoroughly engaged
in the moment, Lydia
doesn't consciously
register the psychological
tremor, and, unaware of it,
fails to question its nature
or origin.

laundromat, and I have to do my laundry, *and* drink coffee. And 'that café' conveniently offers both laundry-doing and coffee-drinking facilities."

Lydia gives Bubbly a sort of smug *see-I-told-you-so* smile.

Bubbly isn't convinced.

YOU GO THERE ONLY ON THE NIGHTS THEY HAVE STANDUP COMEDY.

I hate it when Bubbly has a point.

"Okay, fine. So sometimes I go, and I watch, and I think about it. But not *seriously*! Why would I want to humiliate myself in front of a group of people and try to force them to listen to me, competing with the sounds of the espresso machine, and the spin cycle, and all the people talking—"

YOU MUST DO STANDUP TO BREAK YOURSELF DOWN.

"I'm already having a breakdown! Why don't you tell me to do something that makes sense? Like go to Chase and film myself opening up an account for a new client? Or packing up monetary units?"

YOU *WILL* DO THREE SETS OF COMEDY AT THE CAFÉ.

YOU *WILL* INTERVIEW GIN.

YOU *WILL* INTERVIEW CYNTHIA CLARK-LIN...

YOU *WILL* PERFORM ALL THREE TASKS...*ASKS*...*ASKS*...

And with that, Bubbly begins to drift away.

Lydia watches Bubbly float off, as Bubbly's theme fades away, and the regular lights restore.

Sometimes, her lack of self-awareness is impressive.

Then, with newfound resolve, mixed with a sort of quiet, hysterical terror, Lydia turns to the camera.

And when I wake up, I make some phone calls.

....

END OF ACT ONE

....

ACT TWO

A FEW DAYS LATER.
DAYS 9 – 26.

ACT TWO

SCENE 1

....

Lydia's apartment.
Day 9.

....

GIN, hoodie casual and comfortable in his own skin, turns to look at Lydia; his mind is working. He's troubled and concerned, but steady.

So you are?

I mean, you *definitely* are?

(indicating the camera) **And that's *not* on?**

He listens a moment, then returns to the subject.

Well, how long have you known?

.₀ O o ᴄ ᴄ Oͺᵛᵘᵘ O ᴅ ᶜO₀₀ O ι O O ₒ O ᵘ O O O O ₀ O ι ₒ ᴗͺᴗ O ᴗ O ₒ O ᵘ O ᵘ ᴅ ᵛ ₒ ᴗ ᴗ n O Ϙ ᵛ ᵛ O T O ∙ n O O ᵖ ᴇ ᴩ O ᴄ Ϙ ₒ ᵛ ₒ

She asks herself, again, what she is doing in the same room as this person.

Then she remembers.

He waits, hearing her out.

You should've told me right away. I *wan*na be there for you, Lydia. You never *let me*.

Gin looks at her. His energy shifts.

You are *one* sexy pregnant lady. Wanna fuck?

Oops. Totally not the right thing to say.

(placating) I'm *kidding*, Lydia.

Not that I don't think it could be a good idea...help alleviate the stress...

He notices the camera again.

I think that's on, Lydia. I see a light flashing?

He listens again as she explains.

Ohhhh. Okay.

Well you should just turn it off and save battery power—

(catching himself) And I *should* stop telling you what you *should* do—I know, I know.

(serious, trying to reassure her) Lydia, you're not really dying. You know that, right? You said yourself, Bernie checked you out, there's nothing wrong with you. It was just a dream.

(conceding) Okay, right, so *that* part wasn't just a dream, you *are*

As is so often the case with Gin, Lydia wonders what the man is actually thinking. She suspects he loves her passionately, desperately, and would ultimately do anything for her...

At the same time, she suspects herself of suspecting something that is an utter fantasy, and mocks herself for even entertaining the idea that there might be anything of actual substance between the two of them.

pregnant. But the part where it told you you were *dying, that* part was just a dream. (tenderly) It's always such a drama with you, Lydia—you're always imagining things are worse than they are.

You know this is just like that time when I was still at Chase, and you were being all crazy, convinced that *someone* was hacking into the network and changing *all* the exchange rates—

—Yeah, I know it was me. But it wasn't *all* the exchange rates, that's my point. One exchange rate. *One.* We got a cheaper trip to France out of it, no one got hurt—what's the problem? You can't just...*relax.*

Yes, of course I will help you with this video if that's what you want, but I think this whole idea about you dying is just...in your head.

    A shift; Gin is uncomfortable.

But Lydia. What do you want to do? What do you want *me* to do?

    He waits for her to tell him.

You got the pills already? You didn't *take* them yet though.

Did you?

    A moment passes.

This is—this is bad. I have to tell Sophie.

Tell me—tell me you want me to tell her, and I will.

I haven't told her because you asked me not to, remember?

His allusion to a more carefree and pleasurable moment, fixed in a rapidly receding past, cuts Lydia; but she also enjoys the sharpness of the memory, swoons into it.

Lydia has often resented his easy mobility, his casual maleness, the freedom with which he seems to operate. Could Lydia move with such carelessness through the world?

Lydia recoils internally at the mention of the name; she is obligated now to consider this other human being, to consider her feelings and consider her pain.

ACT TWO

What? When? When did you tell me to tell her?

(brushing it off) Oh, but you didn't mean it that time.

You were joking!

You *weren't*?

What do you mean, "what do I want"? I want what *you* want—I don't know!

You know I've never been able to know what to do. *You* never tell me!

(realizing it's about to get real) Lydia, please don't get upset about this...

No no, Lydia, don't *cry*, baby...listen, let me—

You *wouldn't* be killing our kid! It's not our *kid*, Lydia—there's no kid right now! It isn't anything yet, it's just a collection of cells. You *know* that, you're just being all...crazy hormones lady.

(sudden forcefulness) Well I can't think of it that way. I can't think of it as our kid.

(as if stating the obvious) Because if I thought about it that way, I'd go crazy, if we're not going to go through with it.

Listen, I want to make you feel better. Can you please just—

> Gin notices the camera again.

Can we stop this? At least for right now? I know you're taping this.

She doesn't want to get into this--not again--but once begun, she can't stop.

They fall back into the old habits, slipping into the well-worn grooves. The same conversation happens again and again; time moves forward, but spins in place.

Lydia hears this, a small throwaway comment that hooks her: would he really care at all?

Of course I know it's not on pause, *Gin not that stupid.*

I don't even know what you want me to say—I don't talk to cameras. I'm not your mother, Lydia.

This is me. This is *Gin.*

Can you put the camera away, and can we talk?

This is—this is a lot for me, too.

It's a lot for me to think about.

I want to think about this.

Turn off the camera, Lydia?

Please?

Small throwaway
comments that hook her
seem to be his specialty.

Lydia breaks, at this:
the open expression,
the wounded voice, the
pleading eyes.

SCENE 2

Lydia's apartment.
Moments later.

Gin has left.

LYDIA returns to the camera.

Well, the thing about Manchild—Gin—is, it's always been kind of...bad timing.

Like when we first met, at Chase, we were both kind of...seeing other people. At the time.

And then we both kind of...started seeing each other, too.

(rushing to explain) It wasn't anything at first, he just heard me listening

ᵒᑫᵒ**Ɒ·ᵒᵒ·ᵒᵃᵒᵁᎠᵊ ᵖᵒ ᵊᵁ ᶜᵒ ᵒ ᵤ ᵤ Ɒᵈᵁᵁᵒᵈ ᵆᎠᵒᵊᵒ ᵢᵒᵒ.ᵒ.ᵇᵁᵒᵒᎠ ᵒᵒᵎ ᵎ ᵎᵁᵛᵊᎠᵤᵁᵒᵈ ᵒᎠᵒᵈᵤᵒᵤᵁᵊᵈᵊᵒᵊᵤᵣᵊ Ɒ♋ᵎᵎᵎᵒᵣᵒᵊᎠ ᵒ Ɒᵒᵈ·ᵒᵒ·ᵒᵊᵣᵉ**

It's a terrible, embarrassing, stupid story.

A terrible, embarrassing, stupid story that she sorta loves telling.

Although she wouldn't actually tell you that.

to some old-old Bill Hicks tracks one day, and he told me that Bill Hicks was *his* favorite dead comic who never sold out, too. And we started going to some comedy shows together in the city. And then stuff kind of...*happened*.

And then we felt badly about it! And we *stopped*. Seeing each other.

But, you know, not before we'd completely destroyed the relationships we were already in, beyond all recognition or repair...

And then we kind of hated each other for doing that, or hated ourselves, or something...

And then, you know, some time passed. Gin left the bank, and I stayed— he's always been more of a free agent guy with his I.T. skills, so he can go wherever he wants...

And he doesn't have the same...*commitment* to monetary units that *I* have, so he was okay with leaving.

And I was okay with him leaving! I mean, it was *easier* when we didn't have to see each other *every* day.

And then, a while later, we ran into each other again...just *happened* to wander into the same bar one night—San Francisco kind of sucks, in that respect—it's kind of *hard* to not run into someone you're studiously trying to *avoid* running into—and we couldn't help ourselves from falling back into the same pattern.

But it was bad timing, *again*—see, he'd kind of gotten *engaged*, by that point, and that's just generally a bad time for two people who might potentially want to spend a lot of time together, to meet.

She knows there's no pride in fucking up people's lives, including her own.

Or she knows, at least, that there shouldn't be.

But I guess there's this mutual attraction...or chemistry...or something, right. And stuff just...*happened*. And kept happening. For a while.

Like, it's still happening. Sometimes.

> Something occurs to her: she has another story to tell. This one's good. Ready?

So his name—Gin?

It's a Korean name. For *gold*.

Right???

Gold.

So Gin—*gold*—and *Lydia*—that whole history with the currency and the river of gold...

...I think if I actually carried this thing to term, I'd end up giving birth to a *giant coin*. One big shining monetary unit.

(encountering a snag in the logic) **Although Bubbly doesn't really talk the way I imagine a monetary unit would talk...**

...Well, of course not! It's a *dream*, not anything...

(brushing aside a thought) **But—Gin.**

Well, he's going to be married at some point. Or that's what he says.

So it's never going to work, I guess.

She confesses her participation in another person's infidelities.

A confession that feels more like a boast of sorts.

She just can't help herself.

And once he's married, I can...move on. Or something.

65

> Lydia's attention seems to wander, distracted by how unconvincing this logic seems to be.

Focus, Lydia! Monetary units. Apocalypse. Monetary units. Apocalypse.

> Lydia tries to focus.

> But she resolves to be rational, to articulate a clear understanding of the situation.

> She pats herself on the back for her grand act of acceptance.

> Which of course is in no way a grand act of bad faith.

SCENE 3

Lydia's apartment.
Same day.

Bernie is over at Lydia's, and in a relaxed mood; just the girls hanging out.

BERNIE turns to the camera, laughing, to dish about Lydia.

Oh, *oh*, this one I *gotta* talk about—*to the cam*era.

So one thing Lydia *always* says—aside from boring you to death with her whole history of currency and the wealthy kingdom of Lydia, blahblah*blah*—one thing Lydia *always* says is, "Maybe the apocalypse will come tomorrow."

Like whenever she's worried about something, or she thinks she fucked

Has Lydia really staked her identity on fantasies and catch-phrases?

up, or she's nervous:

"Oh, well, maybe the apocalypse will come tomorrow."

Like when you applied for this job at Chase, right? I remember as *soon* as you interviewed, you were like, (lightly mocking her) "Oh *god*, Bernie, they *hated* me, they probably won't even call me back. Oh well, maybe the apocalypse will come tomorrow."

Right? And save you from the world? Maybe we'll all be saved by the end of the world. Is that right, Lydia?

> Bernie notices the camera, and gives Lydia a conspiratorial look.

(lowering her voice) Hey, am I supposed to be talking about you in the third person? Think your little phantom fetus is gonna get *pissed*, and threaten to kill me, too?

(laughing, but impressed) Holy shit, Lydia, when you go crazy, you really *go crazy.*

Every so often, she is troubled by the thought that what is foundational to her might be viewed by others as fluff.

But Lydia takes pleasure in being teased; at an early age, she learned to associate ridicule with affection, and politeness with indifference.

Make of that what you will.

SCENE 4

A laundromat/coffee shop hybrid establishment.
Day 10.

We hear the sounds of a busy coffee house:

The hissing of an espresso machine, the clattering of ceramic dishes, conversations being carried on at low, and not-so-low, murmurs.

There is a smattering of applause—not the most enthusiastic.

An open mic is in progress.

The HOST of the open mic is at the microphone.

And our next comic is new to the room, and she looks a little nervous. So please give a warm welcome to our first *female* comic of the night, Lydia Clark-Lin, everyone. Come on, make some noise.

LYDIA approaches the microphone with trepidation.

She glances at the audience members with anxiety; the anxiety, however, is controlled, to a degree.

She looks down at a thin stack of index cards in her hands.

The sounds of the café lessen, but continue.

Hi.

My name is Lydia Clark-Lin and I am here against my will, under orders from my developing fetus, who visits me in my sleep and gives me instructions.

She looks around the room, taking in the blank stares.

(moving on quickly, this can still work out) Um, okay, so I anticipated that if I introduced myself in that way, I might receive this kind of response, so I guess that's okay.

I mean, I'm *kidding*, anyway. I don't have a developing fetus talking to me, that would be, like, crazy, right?

It's an embryo, technically. Until the eighth week. And don't worry, it's not gonna make it that long!

There is dead silence; the joke has bombed.

(thrown, addressing the host) I only have five minutes to fill here, right?

Okay, so I tried to write down some notes—

(pulling out some index cards, and promptly dropping them) Oh, sorry—

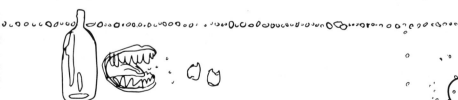

Lydia hears something from the crowd.

What's that?

Oh, yeah, I'll hurry up—

—Huh?

(recovering, sheepish but relieved) Oh, you were *jok*ing.

I get it, that's very funny. You are a very funny audience member. Good job.

Lydia gives the dude a thumbs up.

She hears something from another part of the audience.

What's that?

(embarrassed) Oh, he *wasn't* joking?

Everyone's got something to say. What a participatory audience this is!

Well I'm just gonna start, don't mind me, just carry on with what you're doing—that's right, make that cappuccino, do that laundry, just like that. I've just got a few things to say and then I'll be on my way.

(reading off an index card) My mom is a TV newscaster, so I'm *not* uninformed. Just traumatized.

She waits a moment for laughter...that does not come.

I guess that one's more of an *inside* joke among the children of newscasters.

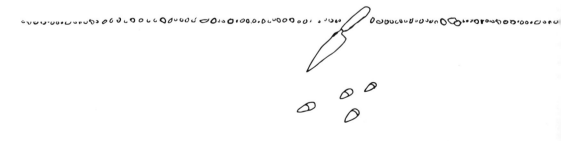

(looking at another card) **My mom tells me my dad is Chinese, and that he left her for an Asian woman when I was still in the womb.**

I was like, "Oh, mom, I guess next time you won't ask to know the sex of the baby first, so your only daughter can grow up with a father figure in her life."

The room is dead silent.

(conceding) **Yeah, I guess that one's kind of convoluted logic, huh.**

It's because there's this stereotype about Asian men preferring boys— (oops) **not sexually! Preferring boys for their** *progeny*—(considering) **I mean, it's not really a stereotype, it's kind of true—**(oops again) **not that all stereotypes are true!** (conceding) **But this one kind of is...**

Great, my first open mic and I'm already perpetuating stereotypes. Good job, Lydia! Maybe the apocalypse will come tomorrow.

(forging ahead; this set has no future, but why not) **So my mom hates Asian women—because you know my dad left her for an Asian woman, right— and that makes things kind of awkward and uncomfortable for the two of us, because...well, you know...**

(gesturing towards her facial features) **Hello!**

(noticing the light; to the host) **That's the third time you've flashed that at me—does that** *mean* **something?**

(chastened but relieved) **Oh, okay,** *got* **it! I am** *leav*ing **the stage.**

ACT TWO   Thanks for, um, listening.

Lydia rushes off.

SCENE 5

Halifax, CA.
Day 11.

Greater Halifax News theme plays as Cynthia prepares to deliver her report.

The music ends, and CYNTHIA turns to the camera.

A group of Halifax residents has mobilized to respond to the introduction of units operated by FPMS—Family Planning Mobile Services—in the area. The group, Halifaxans Organized to Respect Embryonic Sanctity—or HORES, for short—believes that FPMS should be shut down, and that the current law barring abortions after the first third of the first trimester doesn't go far enough. I'm here with HORES co-chair Lindsey Gough. How are you doing today, Ms. Gough?

Cynthia turns to LINDSEY GOUGH, a fragile woman of indeterminate older age. She speaks slowly and deliberately, her manner a blend of sweet-old-lady and severe librarian.

LINDSEY: Oh, that's Hor-*rez*, two syllables, thank you.

CYNTHIA: In recent years, ever since the Supreme Court upheld a ban on a certain form of late-term abortion, we've seen abortion nearly *illegalized* across the country. Tell me, Ms. Gough, why has HORES decided to organize in this way? Haven't you seen the nation coming to your side?

LINDSEY: (sweetly, but firmly) Oh, that's Hor-*rez*, *two* syllables, thank you for making a note of that. The law has not gone far enough in respecting life, and as a country we are ignoring the big old elephant in the room. If the government admits that abortion is a horrific act under some conditions, well then it's obviously admitting that it's horrific, period. Let me give you an example to illustrate what I'm talking about.

CYNTHIA: I'd love that.

LINDSEY: (matter of factly; this is the most reasonable argument in the world) If I were to kill you by peeling off your skin and letting you slowly bleed to death—instead of by simply putting a gun to your head and pulling the trigger—of course having your skin peeled off and slowly bleeding to death may be a more grisly and *prolonged* way of dying, but the bullet's still going to kill you. Now what kind of law would say that it's *not* okay for me to skin you and let you bleed to death, but that it *is* okay for me to put a bullet through your brain?

Lindsey smiles.

CYNTHIA: (with frozen professionalism) What a *fascinating* analogy!

LINDSEY: (continuing) Halifaxans Organized to Respect Embryonic Sanctity are *tired* of watching our tax dollars subsidizing *murder*.

CYNTHIA: But FPMS, the only organized abortion provider in the country, is funded by *private* contributions.

LINDSEY: (sweetly) I don't understand what you're getting at. We are *tired* of watching people trying to rationalize *murder*. This "Death Angel" doctor is a murderer, and we want her behind bars, and her disgusting killing tanks repurposed for something lawful and *civilized*.

Why are we using *armored vehicles* to *kill* innocent *children*, here on *American soil*, when we could be using those armored vehicles in Iran? And North Korea?

CYNTHIA: But the vehicles operated by FPMS were deemed militarily obsolete by the United States government.

LINDSEY: I don't see your point.

CYNTHIA: So what are the next steps for HORES?

LINDSEY: (one time too many, but we can still be reasonable here) That's Hor-*rez*. Thank you for correcting that the next time you say it unless you want a little surprise visit from one of our operatives.

We intend to mobilize specially trained volunteers to go out and find abortion workers, and enforce our own sense of justice, while we wait for the law to catch up.

CYNTHIA: I guess Halifax residents should be on the lookout for HORES—

ACT TWO   LINDSEY: (furious, correcting) *Rez!*

CYNTHIA: Sounds like we'll be seeing a *lot* of you in the future.

(turning towards the camera) This is Cynthia Clark-Lin, with *Greater Halifax News.* Back to you.

Greater Halifax News outro plays; lights out.

SCENE 6

Lydia's apartment.
Day 12.

BERNIE is lying on her back, arms behind her head, staring at the ceiling.

She's had a long week. She laughs.

You know, I'm actually getting kind of used to this?

She turns to talk directly into the camera.

Hello, viewers of "Lydia's Funeral Video." It's me, Bernadette Tayag, aka the Bay Area's "Death Angel."

No really, Lydia, I *like* doing this. It's kind of...therapeutic. I think your

Lydia wants a super-hero name, too: she finds it hard to believe that Bernie really resents her notoriety as much as she claims to.

Deep down, Lydia thinks, Bernie must love the fact that she's a public figure of enough significance to merit her own special name.

ACT TWO

deranged imagination actually had a good idea this time around.

By the way, Lydia, you completed the termination treatment, right?

(alarmed) You haven't taken the pills yet?

But Lydia, you've only got two and a half weeks left—you *know* that, right?

Have you changed your mind about this? Are you thinking you want to go through with the pregnancy after all?

> She listens a moment.

(her training kicked in) Are you sure?

(patient and reassuring) Because you know it's as much your choice to let the pregnancy continue, as it is to terminate it.

> Bernie hears Lydia out, nodding.

Okay.

(abandoning her training) Then what the fuck are you *waiting* for? Like I *told* you, I can help you with this only within the twenty-eight day *window*, alright? You know how *hard* it was to hold on to those twenty-eight *days*?

> She allows Lydia to answer.

Good. You better. Hah!

> Bernie takes a moment to regain her cool.

ᵒᵖᵒᵒᵒᵒᵒᵒᵒᵒᵒᵘᵒᵖᵎ ᵖᵒᵎᵒᵒᵒ ᵒᵘ ᵘ ᵒᵒᵘᵘᵒᵘ ᵒᵒᵘᵘᵒᵎᵒᵎᵒᵘ·ᵒᵘᵒᵒᵒ ᵒᵒᵎ · ᵎᵒᵘᵒᵘ ᵒᵖ ᵘᵘᵘᵘᵘ ᵘᵒᵘ ᵒᵒᵖᵎᵎᵒᵖᵒᵘᵖ ᵒᵖᵒᵒᵒᵒᵒᵘ

| It's rough, being significant to the world. | And it's rough, when your not-so-significant-but-still-best friend refuses to complete the simplest of tasks. | Lydia resents the fact that Bernie is handling her with kid gloves; she doesn't need to be super-supported or counseled like she's a frightened teenager, thank you very much. | But she also resents being lectured to; she doesn't need that, either. |

I'm just a little stressed, Lydia.

I was in Halifax today, setting up the new unit, right? And there's this group of twenty, twenty-five people, shoving these huge video placards in my face, showing these second and third trimester fetuses getting all mangled up in some botched up back-alley abortion procedure. They probably got the video from one of those Craigslist doctors who don't know what the *fuck* they're doing, just know people are desperate and want to make some cash—and I'm like, "Bitches, *you*'re responsible for that shit. Now I am *trying* to work, will you leave me the fuck alone and just let people decide what happens to the cells in their own bodies? Are you gonna start protesting every fucking surgery to remove breast tumors? Because those *are* living cells, too, those cancer cells. Same DNA."

Stupid people. Screaming at me, scaring the shit out of my patients.

Bernie's anger is broken by a new thought; she laughs.

You know, I wish I could abort *them,* Lydia.

I would *love* to be like, "Shut the fuck up bitch, I will *abort* you!"

(as if shooting a gun) **Backa-backa!** "How's *that* for a late-term abortion?" Hah!

She breaks off a moment, brooding.

They just have me stressed *out.*

They're called—(finding the humor again) **get this, Lydia, they're HORES—**

No, no, they actually *call* themselves HORES! Not "whores" like we-get-

Lydia senses an unfamiliar something in Bernie's mood.

Unfamiliar...and unsettling.

She is relieved when Bernie relaxes again into joking; she doesn't quite know how to respond when her heroic warrior friend's spirits are depressed.

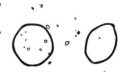

paid-for-sexual-services whores; "HORES" like my-organization-has-a-dumb-ass-acronym HORES.

I forget what it stands for...(making it up as she goes along)...Hypocrites Obsessed with...Retarded Ethics...and Stupidity—no that's not it. Your mother would know—have you seen her lately?

A moment passes.

(serious) Have you *talked* to her?

Lydia, call your mother. Call your mother, Lydia! She'd love to hear from you. Damn Lydia, I talk to your mother more than *you* do—

—Yeah I know it's because she *has* to interview me, but *still*. I *see* her. We *talk*.

Believe me, she misses you.

Bernie listens to Lydia a moment.

Well, no, not in those exact words, but you know, I can read between the lines.

Like whenever she says, "Dr. Tayag is based in San Francisco," I know that she's also thinking, "...San Francisco, where my beloved daughter who never calls me also resides."

You never see her. You should be grateful you have a mother who will *talk* to you, and didn't *disown* you because you're known as the "Death Angel," alright?

(pulling on her jacket) So call your mother, Lydia. It's crazy in Halifax.

At the mention of Bernie's rapport with her mother, Lydia feels the old jealousy flare up for a moment.

Inwardly, Lydia wishes the conversation hadn't taken this turn.

Sure, she has to take it in stride on the camera, but...

...she *needs* you.

Bernie gives Lydia an *I-mean-it* look, and she's out.

SCENE 7

Cynthia's home in Halifax.
Day 13.

A somewhat apprehensive CYNTHIA is tidying up. The doorbell rings.

She freezes at the sound.

Then, quickly composing herself, she opens the door.

Oh my, well look who finally decided to make an appearance.

Cynthia moves to embrace Lydia, but is rebuffed.

Cynthia absorbs this; after a moment, she follows Lydia into the house, proceeding coolly:

Lydia has always reflexively winced at the rare moments her mother attempts physical contact; she finds any overture of warmth to be suspect.

Well, Lydia, I don't know why you took it upon yourself to drive all the way out here. I don't *need* to see you, after all.

I've gotten *used* to not seeing you, after all these years of you not coming to see me.

> Cynthia notices something about Lydia; her expression changes.

What's wrong? There's something wrong.

Of *course* there's something wrong, you think I can't tell?

(reassuming her controlled air of unconcern) **Fine, don't tell me, I don't *need* to know.**

(brusquely) **And I can't talk long, I am a *bit* busy—busy with a capital *B*— trying to cover all the activity in Halifax these days.**

But Bernadette talked me into it, and I've always had such a soft spot for that girl—

—Well that's just ridiculous, of course I don't *really* think of her as the Death Angel. I can't help what the locals say, I just report the news.

But she is *such* an impressive woman, always working. The way the two of you were so inseparable growing up, well...

> She sweeps her eyes over Lydia in an appraising manner.

...it's a *wonder* you didn't turn out more a*like*...

Well, of course you work hard, too—of course you do! Assisting the

Halifax is just a quick drive across the bridge, but there's always some reason or other. And her mother's always so busy.

Lydia is both surprised by and resentful of her mother's sharp eye. Why is it that Lydia doesn't seem to have inherited any of her mother's good qualities? What, in fact, did she inherit from her mother at all?

Lydia resolves to say nothing; she refuses to give her mother the satisfaction of being right. At this reflexive, and petulant, thought, Lydia wonders, again, if she will be forever a fifteen-year-old in her mother's presence.

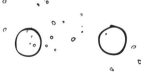

machines in their automated task of dispensing cash—that's *very* important.

Maybe not as important as pursuing your *talents*, Lydia—and you certainly have them *somewhere*, you *are* my daughter after all—but I guess pursuing your talents just isn't your *thing*, for some deranged reason. (almost under her breath) **You must have gotten that from your father...**

A moment as Cynthia observes Lydia and the camera.

Well. This is beginning to feel...awkward.

Maybe we've said a lot to each other's faces, Lydia, but I don't like the idea of being edited down to some Mother caricature for a video in which *you* are lionized, and *I* end up coming across as the...idiot *racist*, hmm? Who could never *bond* with her daughter?

You know that's the thing, Lydia, a *lot* of people don't *bond* with their children, it's not about *race*. And you always, *always*—(anticipating an interruption)—ah-ah-ah, *wait*, I'm not finished—you always, *always*, boil it down to race.

You think that just because my *daughter* is a woman of *color*—yes, see, I can use your terminology with *facility* alright?—You think that just because my daughter is a *P.O.C*....

She gives Lydia a self-satisfied smile for knowing this term, too.

...and *I* am a white woman, that I'm *ignorant*, and that everything that goes wrong is *my* fault.

And *now* you're going off making this *childish* video celebrating *you* for

Awkward, indeed.

Her mother, Lydia thinks, has an interesting way of relating to issues of race. Interesting, in that she seems to resent issues of race being issues at all.

Of course in emphatically asserting the non-issueness of race, she winds up demonstrating exactly the opposite.

And how morbid is *that* by the way? Just to go into every *tragic* little detail of your *tragic* little life?

Darling, I hate to point this out to you, but you didn't *have* a tragic little life. If you want to be *tragic*, I'm afraid you're going to have to do a *bit* more than complete an unremarkable undergraduate degree at State, and enlist in an uninspiring job. That may be...*pathetic*, but it's not *tragic*.

I know it's *on*, Lydia, I can sense a camera running from a mile away.

> Cynthia smiles, repositions herself, and gazes confidently at the camera.

So! You want me to talk about you, do you? Well...

> She searches a moment.

You were always a very...*showy*...personality. *Very* talented—you used to write the most *captivating* stories...when you were younger. *Everyone* enjoyed them.

I think it was the influence of seeing *me* in my role as newscaster: (direct look into the lens) Cynthia Clark-Lin of *Greater Halifax News*.

Cynthia Clark-Lin, now *that's* a name that really *pops* out at you. That's why I kept your father's part of the name in there, you know—I couldn't very well go back to being plain old *Cynthia Clark* just because *he* left, now could I? Besides, you've got half his genes, and you were here to stay. So, leave the name the way it is! It's easier that way.

I've got better things to do than be bitter over the past, Lydia. Because

C Clerk-Lin
Clerk ~~Lin~~
Clerk ~~Clerk~~
Clark

Again, at the allusion to her childhood pursuits, Lydia experiences the familiar blend of pleasure and sting.

She was so much more interesting, she thinks, as an eight-year-old.

as someone who reports the news, I have to always be *on*. I have to always show my face to the world—my *good* face—and I can never break.

These days, people just subscribe to the *feeds* online, and read their *blog*lines—news by third or fourth or *fifth* party—and fewer people are watching *real* news, brought to you by a *real* person.

And that's key. That a *human being* is reporting it, to you, in your living room—or at a diner, or at an airport—live news is very *very key*.

It's just like when a friend tells you a story about something going on in her life. That's not a clinical display; that's a human *connection*. And that's what *I'm* doing. I'm that friend, that trusted friend, telling you a *story*. Providing that *connection*.

And I'd like to say, Lydia—since you always like to *ridicule* me for being in the local *obsolete* TV news—sure, maybe I'd love to be in the national networks someday, but local is where it *starts*, Lydia. You think national news is just *suddenly* national news? No! it always starts *some*where.

Like right now: this Halifax group going around with their *crazy* referendum? *That's* going to sweep the nation. All trends start small with a group of crazies, and then they go *huge*.

So you'd better pay attention to what's happening in Halifax, Lydia. Because the ugly in Halifax is going to become the ugly in San Francisco.

What?

Oh, I'm sorry, you wanted me to talk about *you*. That's right, because it's always about you.

Has she really never seen her mother break? What would it look like if she ever did?

As her mother launches into yet another sermon about the power of live news, Lydia rolls her eyes; a gesture of disdain to bolster herself against any feelings akin to admiration.

Please, she will *never* make it to national. Dream on, lady.

Hearing the sarcasm of this unbidden thought, Lydia is surprised by a sudden, and mortifying, rush of sympathy, which she quickly stanches.

Sorry, I'm sorry I actually talked about the *world*, for a moment, and didn't just talk about *you* the entire time.

Oh lighten up, Lydia, you have *got* to relax. It's always such a drama with you!

But who am I to judge after all?

I'm just a *white* woman who can't understand her *multiracial* daughter.

Cynthia laughs.

So much for a quick drive across the bridge.

SCENE 8

Laundromat/coffee shop hybrid establishment.
Day 15.

We hear the same ambient café sound as before.

The HOST is at the microphone.

And our next comic is originally from Halifax—you *sure* you want to be sharing that information, honey? (laughs)—and she was here last week.

We all thought she was...just great.

So please give it up for Lydia Clark-Lin, everyone.

Come on, come on, let's hear it, give her a chance.

This isn't easy folks, come on.

LYDIA approaches the microphone, more determined than the last time.

She plunges in with bravado and resentment:

This is the second time I've done this. So I only have to do it one more time. Which is great.

So you know how when you have a developing embryo talking to you and giving you instructions, it can be, like, really hard to focus?

It's like, "Look, honey, you haven't even been *born* yet, and you're *already* trying to control my life? Keep that up and you're *never* getting out of there. You'll be getting a visit from Mr. Coat Hanger!"

Eek. Dead silence as the ambient sound cuts out.

(losing her confidence somewhat) Sorry, wrong crowd? You don't think threatening a fetus is funny?

I guess I misunderstood, I've been sitting in the back for the last two hours listening to dick jokes and how hilarious the idea of being gay is, so I guess I thought your standards weren't that high.

Lydia seems to remember that she doesn't really give a shit anymore.

She forges ahead recklessly:

So I'm two weeks pregnant, and when I found out I was pregnant, I was like, "Oh no, I guess it's time to make some *major* lifestyle changes. Because a miscarriage isn't gonna happen without a little help."

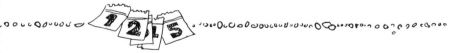

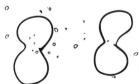

ACT TWO

I'm thinking drink a lot of alcohol, smoke a lot of cigarettes, have my boyfriend push me down the stairs a few times a week. You know, take care of myself.

I'm kidding. I don't have a boyfriend.

He's a fiancé. Not mine, someone else's. But we get along great when he's not getting me pregnant.

I'm excited about being pregnant, though. I mean, who *doesn't* dream of one day terminating an unplanned pregnancy? It's like a medical fun pass.

Actually, the whole process can be kind of, you know, emotional. But I can't really call up my boss and say, "Hey, I'm dealing with the emotional and financial detritus of terminating an unplanned pregnancy, I need to take some time off."

See, if I were getting a heart transplant, it'd be a different story:

"Sure, sure, I totally understand, take all the time you need."

People getting a heart transplant *really* have it easy in this country, don't they? *Every*one's lining up to throw you a fundraiser to help pay for your medical expenses.

So far, no one's really donated to the Help Lydia Abort Her Embryo Fund. HLAHEF. I've got a Kickstarter, check it out.

Okay, um, a lot of my friends are worried because abortion is being outlawed across the country, and ever since Planned Parenthood shut down, they're like, (whiny voice) "Oh no, we're losing all our rights, we

won't be able to terminate our pregnancies any more." You know, whining and shit, the way the ladies do?

I'm not as worried, though. Because I think maybe that could be a good thing. People in this country, women especially, we have to step up and take more responsibility for our actions and *stop* aborting our babies.

And *start* abandoning them. On a church step, in a dumpster, a picnic basket, whatever—

Lydia spots something offstage.

Oh, there's that light again! Well, thanks for listening.

Lydia looks at the audience for a beat, and leaves the microphone.

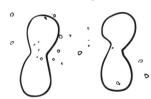

SCENE 9

*In front of the Halifax FPMS unit.
Day 16.*

We hear sounds of a protest, and angry shouting from the crowd:

"Stop killing babies!", "Get out of Halifax!", "God's going to punish you!",
"Baby killer!", etc.

The *Greater Halifax News* theme plays as CYNTHIA navigates the
crowd, heading toward Bernie's FPMS unit.

The music concludes, and Cynthia's on, standing next to Bernie, raising
her voice to be heard over the crowd.

BERNIE is courteous, but drives through the interview with fluency and
professionalism, eager to get back to work.

CYNTHIA: I'm here with Dr. Bernadette Tayag outside her new Family Planning Mobile Services unit here in Halifax. How are you doing today, Dr. Tayag?

BERNIE: Well, we've faced some challenges, but overall I'm satisfied with our progress.

CYNTHIA: Could you describe some of the challenges you've faced here in Halifax?

BERNIE: Well, Cynthia, as you know, there's been some resistance to the FPMS unit in the area, and we've encountered some very hostile protesters outside of the clinic. Apparently, some people—a small, but very *vocal*, minority—still actually believe that individuals should not have the right to choose.

CYNTHIA: And what do *you* believe? That a woman can choose? Life or death?

BERNIE: (after an almost imperceptible pause) A terminated pregnancy *isn't* a death.

CYNTHIA: Of course it's not. Do you feel there's a need for FPMS units in the area?

BERNIE: There's a need for them everywhere in this country.

CYNTHIA: That sounds a little extreme, even coming from a pro-abortion extremist like yourself.

BERNIE: Cynthia, in the last decade, the number of women killed during

an abortion has tripled, primarily due to the proliferation of unlicensed "doctors" operating in unsafe and unregulated environments. FPMS offers safe, regulated, and affordable services. Unfortunately, no one else is doing that right now, not since Planned Parenthood closed its doors.

CYNTHIA: And what about women who aren't sure? Who have doubts about whether or not it's wrong to terminate a pregnancy? What do you say to them?

After a flicker of hesitation, Bernie continues, firmly:

BERNIE: I don't offer psychological counseling; I'm a medical doctor.

CYNTHIA: (name-check to the camera) And *I'm* Cynthia Clark-Lin.

An awkward silence hangs in the air a moment before Cynthia cheerfully resumes:

CYNTHIA: (back to Bernie) I hear you wear a bulletproof vest.

BERNIE: (recovering her confidence) All FPMS staff wear bulletproof vests.

CYNTHIA: And that's all the time we have for today. It's been great speaking with you, Doctor Tayag.

(to the carmera) This is Cynthia Clark-Lin, with *Greater Halifax News*.

The camera cuts out.

SCENE 10

Lydia's apartment.
Day 17.

KIMMIE has just arrived for another interview; she sits down eagerly, beaming.

Yay-yay-*yay*! I'm *so* glad we're doing this again, I thought I did it *wrong* last time, you stopped so ab*ru*ptly.

(waving into the camera) *Hiiii!*

Is it on? It's on? Okay, I just want to make sure it's on.

(waving again at camera) Hiiii. Hi everyone, it's *Kimmie* again.

Lydia recalibrates, instinctively dialing down her natural level of expressiveness in an attempt to counterbalance Kimmie's inescapable exuberance.

ACT TWO

She smiles at the camera.

She waits a moment, staring.

(to Lydia) **So what should I say?**

Before Lydia can respond, Kimmie suddenly remembers something.

We've been trying to *call* you, Lydia, haven't you been getting John's messages? We thought you got much *sicker* or something, or that you were like maybe even in the *hospital* or something!

He said—he *told* me, (carefully repeating his words, so she doesn't make any mistakes) "If she hasn't called back yet after *all* this time, then she better be *in* a coma, *on* life support, *at* the hospital."

Kimmie waits a quick moment before barreling ahead:

He's *really* really concerned.

We miss you! It's so dry and boring without Lydia stories!

We were in this training for this new optical scanning equipment the other day—because now everyone opening a new account has to get an optical scan, not just the merchant clients anymore—and the trainer stepped out of the room, and we were just directing the optical scanner at random things, like a coke can, or Ben's turkey sandwich (laughs), you know, just to see how it would register in the machine? Like in comparison to an actual *eye*?

Doesn't that sound like it would be a lot of fun? We thought it would be a *lot* of fun.

A part of her quiets to compensate; it has to. It's like a law of conservation of total social energy or something, she thinks.

She feels herself becoming more remote, watching now from some distance off.

Watching Kimmie, watching herself watching.

There is nothing for her to say.

(suddenly solemn, considering) But there was just something *missing*, somehow. It wasn't really that fun.

(rallying her spirits) And then someone said, "Too bad *Lydia's* not here, she'd know how to make the most out of our *alone* time with the *optical scanner.*"

And we all *laughed*, because that was so *true*...(wistfully) You totally, *totally*, would've known what to do with the optical scanner...

> Kimmie nods silently a moment in agreement with herself.

You should call John back. He'd *so* so want to hear from you.

(eager for more prompts) So what else should I say?

> The camera shuts off.

It's like she's not even there anymore.

SCENE 11

Lydia's apartment.
Day 19.

LYDIA is alone, thinking something over.

After a few moments, her eyes are drawn to the camera.

When she speaks, she is somewhat uncertain and distracted.

Last night, Bubbly talked to me again.

The Bubbly theme plays, and the lights transition into the dream space.

The tangle of blue lights begins to glow softly, although Lydia never looks at it directly.

∘ᵒᴑᴑ·ᴑᴑ·ᴑ∿ᴑᴑᴈ ᴑᴑ ᴈ ᴖ ᴑ ᴑ ᴖ ᴖ Ꙩᴈᴖᴖᴑᴈ ᴑᴕᴈᴈᴑ ᴦᴑᴑ₀ᴑ·ᴑ ᴖᴖᴕᴑᴕᴑᴑᴈ ᴑᴑᴦ ᴈ ᴈ ᴖᴖᴈᴕᴑᴑ ᴑᴑᴑ ᴑ ᴑ ᴕ ᴑ ᴈ ᴑ ᴖ ᴑ ᴈ ᴑ ᴑ ᴖᴑᴈᴑ ᴈ ᴖ ᴖᴑ Ꙩᴈ ᴖ ᴖ ᴖ ᴦ ᴑ ᴖ ᴖ ᴑ ᴑ ᴑ ᴑ · ᴑ ᴑ · ᴑ ᴑ ᴦ

She would like to have
some clarity.

(seeing what she saw in her dream) **It was different.**

It looked...human. It came to me looking human.

And I said, "You know, that's kind of, um, not ideal, for you to come to me looking that way."

And Bubbly says:

I'M AN EXPRESSION OF HUMAN CONSCIOUSNESS,
I CAN APPEAR IN WHATEVER FORM I CHOOSE.

Well, look who's being all superior and pulling rank.

And I say, "Yeah, but...Well, I know I haven't taken the pills yet, but I still have a week and a half left to take them, and I thought I was *terminating* this pregnancy."

And Bubbly says:

YOU WILL TERMINATE THE PREGNANCY, YES.

And I say, "So it's difficult for me to...*deal*...with that decision. To terminate this pregnancy, and to terminate *you*, when you start *looking* like a *human*."

And Bubbly says:

I WAS ALREADY TALKING TO YOU AS A MATURE CONSCIOUSNESS,
WHAT DIFFERENCE DOES IT MAKE WHAT I LOOK LIKE?

Lydia makes an *are-you-fucking-kidding-me?* expression.

The whole mystery-and-murk of dreamworlds is getting old.

But will the mystery and murk disappear when she wakes up?

ACT TWO   It makes—it makes a difference!

It was *already* hard. Because...

(struggling to make a point) You know, I've been *very good* about doing what you say. I've even kind of *enjoyed* it a little. Talking to Bernie and Gin, humiliating myself in front of a group of strangers...that was *fun*. Once I realized I didn't have much of a choice—do what the embryo says or lose your sanity for good. And I mean it's not like you're telling me to go out and stab someone or blow up a building or anything, so you're obviously not some evil thing in my head. *I'm* the only one dying here.

But I mean (genuine confusion) I was doing everything right. So why did you have to push it? By doing this? By looking like this?

So I am—I am conflicted.

> Lydia stops, waiting for Bubbly to help her out.
>
> Bubbly doesn't.

YOU HAVE TEN DAYS TO FINISH THE VIDEO AND TERMINATE THE PREGNANCY.

And then Bubbly floats away.

And standing in the desert, watching Bubbly drift into the horizon....

> She looks around her, seeing it happen:

...the sand gives way to salt water, and I'm adrift in an endless sea.

And I sink into a new unconsciousness under a canopy of stars.

᠊᠊᠊

The clarity of consciousness   It's all indecipherable   ...desert and ocean...
is a fantasy.   wilderness...

Stars begin to glow as Bubbly theme fades out.

Unknowable.

SCENE 12

Lydia's apartment.
Day 21.

GIN has just heard Lydia's most recent dream.

He seems slightly on edge, pacing around as he talks to her.

It looked human?

He considers a moment.

Well, what kind of human?

He listens.

Gin sometimes surprises
Lydia by his genuine
interest in pursuing a line
of inquiry...

I mean, was it a baby human? An adult human? Boy or girl?

> Gin takes the answer in, smiling.

Sounds like it can't make up its mind.

Did it look like me?

> Again, Gin takes in her answer, processing it.

So basically we created some kind of...baby Mystique.

(slightly impatient that he has to explain) Mystique, the X-Man who can take on the form of other people? The shape-shifter? You're saying that this thing looked like me, and you, and Bernie, and your mom, at all ages? *Mystique.*

Why are you telling me this, Lydia? I told you I can't think of it that way. It's gone, so—

> Lydia interrupts to correct him.

> Gin is thrown, surprised.

(with a hint of alarm) You haven't taken the pills yet? But don't you—isn't there only a week left?—

—No, no, that's fine if you haven't taken them, that's fine. Just tell me what you want—

> He listens a moment, then speaks:

(with resolve) Okay, listen, Lydia. Whether or not you want to go through with this...

Even a line of inquiry that others might immediately dismiss.

He sometimes surprises her with the seriousness of his questions.

And then sometimes he doesn't surprise her at all.

He takes a breath; he's been wanting to get this out since he arrived.
He speaks haltingly, struggling to articulate his thoughts:

...things are different now. For me.

Since we met each other and started...hanging out, things have always
been...complicated. There's always been this...obstacle.

So with what's happened...I've been thinking these last few days, and I
realized:

I don't want there to be any obstacles any more. I want things to be clear.
For *us*.

He takes another deep breath.

So I told Sophie about you. About us.

I think we're done.

I told her it had to be over between her and me.

He pauses a moment as if he's presented her with a gift and is waiting
for her to open it.

You see? You understand what I'm saying?

(smiling, anticipating her approval) So now...there are no obstacles...

Gin retreats slightly, acknowledging the outstanding complications:

I know it can't be like right away, everything will be perfect. Things are
gonna be really bad for a while—things are really bad right now between

Sometimes he does   Pushes her off balance.   Says something she's not
exactly what she expects.   prepared to hear.

Sophie and me, and I need to make sure she's okay...

But still, *we* can—now *we* can actually try...when we're ready, we could...
we could try again.

If you want me to be ready now, I can be ready now.

Things can be clear for us. Right?

Right, Lydia?

> A moment passes.
>
> Gin is confused by her lack of response.

Lydia?

> He looks at her a moment. The clip ends.

Throws something she's
not prepared to catch.

SCENE 13

Greater Halifax News desk.
Later that night.

Over *GHN* music indicating breaking news, CYNTHIA turns to the camera to deliver a special update, her expression solemn:

In the latest of a series of alarming incidents, another riot broke out in downtown Halifax today when a group of unidentified individuals interrupted an orderly protest in the Verizon Mall parking lot, where private abortion provider and mobile clinic FPMS has been providing services.

The group, which wore ski masks and held signs decrying FPMS, smashed in the windows of five cars and set one vehicle on fire.

One woman was injured and is reportedly in stable condition at Halifax General.

A letter sent to this station claimed responsibility for the riot and promised further violence if FPMS continues service in Halifax.

The letter was signed by the vigilante division of Halifax-based group, (carefully emphasizing the second syllable) Hor-*rez*, Halifaxans Organized to Respect Embryonic Sanctity.

This is Cynthia Clark-Lin, with *Greater Halifax News*.

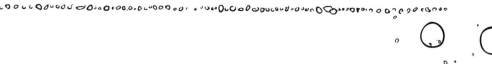

SCENE 14

Lydia's apartment.
Day 22.

BERNIE storms in, furious.

Spotting Lydia, she immediately turns on her, deadly serious.

Lydia, I am going to stab you if you don't turn off that camera.

She waits.

Okay, fine. You want to leave it on, leave it on.

I am *pissed*, Lydia. I am literally fighting off crazy people determined to take this country back a hundred years, and you're *sitting* there, on your

Lydia feels a
stubbornness set in.

pills, *not* taking them. *Why*? When you *can*? You're just gonna piss away the six days you have left, until you can't *do* it anymore? And if you do they'll charge you with a felony? And charge *me* with *multiple* felonies, for assisting in an *illegal* abortion?

Damnit, Lydia, I'm your friend, I support what you do, but I have *had* it with you being so relentlessly *crazy*.

You do *not* have a three-week old embryo *talking* to you! You think it would be *conscious*? You think it would know words like "funeral video"? Where do you think this is coming from?

It's in your *head*, Lydia. You are *dreaming*. You are having *convincing* dreams, but they're dreams. And you are fucking over your life because of some *stupid dream*.

Bernie paces a moment, fuming, then turns back to Lydia again.

You know what this is about?

Your obsession with the apocalypse.

(over Lydia's objection) **Yes, *obsession*.**

(mocking her) "Maybe the apocalypse will come tomorrow, maybe the apocalypse will come tomorrow." Maybe the apocalypse will come tomorrow and save you from all the things you *did*, and all the things you *never* did. You keep focusing on wishing there'd be an apocalypse so you wouldn't have to *think* anymore. So you wouldn't have to keep looking for some kind of *justification* for living. Well you want to know the truth, Lydia?

We *are* on the brink of apocalypse. The world *is* falling apart. Have you

She's tired of being chastised.

Being blamed. Analyzed.

Tired of being held responsible.

looked around you? ...The war in Iran, and now North Korea? Tornadoes in Alaska? World rule by Verizon and Facespace?

And look at Halifax, Lydia—it's burning to the ground.

No, not *literally* burning. *Figuratively.* Damnit, Lydia, you know why I do this, right? Why I do what I do?

Because I see—I see *so clearly*—that certain people, certain *interests*, are trying to control things, to take control away from people who are *already* struggling.

Here we are, going *backwards*. Planned Parenthood—*gone*.

Fuck, Lydia, you think I *like* operating fucking *armored vehicles*?

> She listens a moment before continuing, far from amused:

That's very funny, Lydia, but no, for your information, it's *not* fun. It's *not* like a big video game.

> Bernie thinks, talking herself through it.

I don't see enough people fighting back.

It's all about managing our tolerance and managing our outrage. They push us in small steps, one compromise at a time. We may experience some shock at first, so then they wait...they let us acclimate...and then they push *again*, another notch backwards.

And it all starts in places like Halifax. It all starts with little collections of *crazy* in Halifax.

ɔ◦ᗡ◦ᗡ◦ᐟ◦◦◦ᗡᵎᕐᶸᗡᵎ ᗡ◦ᗡᵕ◦ᗡ◦ᵕᵕ Qᵈᵕᵕᗡᵕ ᗡO◦ᵎᗡ◦◦O◦◦◦◦ᵕᵕᗡᗡ◦◦ᵎ ᵎ ᵎᗡᵎᵎQᵕᗡ◦ᗡᵕᗡᵕᵕᵕᵈᵕᵎᵎᗡᵎᗡᵕᵕ◦Q☾ᵎᵎᗡᵎᗡᵕᵎᗡᗡᗡ◦◦◦◦ᗡᵎᵈ

And would it really be so terrible if it did burn to the ground?	Would it really be so terrible if all of it went down, leaving nothing of the embarrassing awfulness of living but a cool, quiet pile of nonjudgmental ashes?

Bernie listens a moment, then turns on Lydia, completely fed up.

Maybe the apocalypse will come tomorrow, Lydia? Your problem is that you don't recognize an apocalypse when you see one.

I'm done with this, turn that thing off. For real.

Bernie stares at Lydia, waiting for her to turn off the camera.

But Bernie has stopped talking to her, for the moment; she's dropped into that internal place, a place of coiled power and concentration.

A place Lydia can never even hope to enter.

SCENE 15

··

Lydia's apartment.
Moments later.

··

Bernie has just left.

Trying to acknowledge but laugh off Bernie's accusations, LYDIA addresses the camera. A bit defensively:

I am not *obsessed* with the apocalypse.

Of course I see there are *problems* in the world.

Well, I think that Bernie has this kind of "I'm gonna save the world" complex. I mean, I think she can get a little shrill about it, sometimes. A little shrill, and a little self-righteous.

ᵒᴰᵒᴰᵎᵒᵒᵎᶜᵎᵃᴖᴖᴰᵎ ᵖᵈ ᴑᶜᴰᵒᶜᶜ ᴖᵈᵘᵘᵒᴖ ᵎᴖᵎᵎᵒᵎᵒᵒᵎᵒᵎᴖᵘᵒᵒᵒ ᵒᵒᶥ ᵎ ᵎᵘᵘᴖᶜᴖᵈᴖᵘᵘᶜᵘᵘᴖᵎᵒᵘᵘ◯⦾ᵘᵘᵒᵒᵒᵘᴖᵒᴰᵎᵒᵒᵎᶜᵘ

She would like to simply   She would like to simply   TAP   But instead she lashes out.
admire courage.   admire strength.   T AP
                                                       TA P

So yeah, it's great that she's doing these things—running these tanks as abortion clinics, and getting services to women who couldn't get them any other way, and being under fire for the work she's doing the entire time—I mean, sure, I guess, if you use the right *words*—if you *spin* it the right way—it *sounds* like she's doing some kind of heroic deed.

(sheepishly conceding) Okay, so she's doing some kind of heroic deed. I *know* that.

But I mean, she doesn't even *question* it. Maybe she should question what she's doing, too, right? Or what, she just *roams* around, free of indecision, free of doubt, never wondering if she's wrong? Living with *absolute conviction*?

> Lydia thinks about that for a moment.

I wish I could live that way.

But the point is, I am not *obsessed* with the apocalypse, okay?

I say, "Maybe the apocalypse will come tomorrow," because…because… Because maybe it *will*. Maybe the apocalypse *will* come tomorrow.

(suddenly angry) Maybe I just think it's a fun thing to say, alright?

> Lydia turns to leave…

To not do so…

To simply admire without identifying some underlying flaw…

That wouldn't work.

SCENE 16

Lydia's apartment.
Immediately after.

GIN storms in, confronting Lydia.

Why haven't you called—

—I've been...things haven't been...that good...these last few days. Soph—

He stops himself; Sophie's not relevant right now.

Did you take the pills yet?

He waits for her response.

⌁⌁

Lydia doesn't feel up to
fielding a lot of irrelevant
questions.

But I thought—I thought you didn't want it. I thought we *agreed* you weren't going to have it. That's what you kept telling me.

> Gin waits for Lydia to say something. She doesn't. He hesitates, uncertain about what he is about to say.

Sophie wants to stay together—she wants me to stop seeing you.

(genuine anguish) I *did*, I *did* tell her I wanted to be with you, remember? But you didn't call back. I waited a long time. Five days...It *feels* like a really long time.

How could I not see her? Especially when you weren't talking to me? She was so upset.

It doesn't matter anymore. You don't—

> He cuts himself off.

> He starts again, desperate to understand.

I told you I ended things with her, and you disappeared—

(sudden anger) Well, we wouldn't have gotten right back together again if you had called me back.

(confused) You always told me it was just because there was...this obstacle.

And then I removed that obstacle. I told you I removed the obstacle. For us.

But you disappeared. For five days.

> Lydia has no response.

Or indulging someone's efforts to characterize himself as the injured party, the guy with no choices.

Someone who's always blaming someone else, always making it someone else's decision...

A thought occurs to Gin.

He looks at Lydia as if he's just realized something very obvious.

You always wanted the obstacle.

That obstacle, that wasn't an obstacle, was it...

...That was the only reason you were...

Not needing to complete his thought out loud, he turns to go.

Then he stops; he has one more question:

Would you even have been with me in the first place if you had thought it could ever work out?

The question hangs there for a moment.

Lydia doesn't respond.

Gin goes.

...Someone who's always refusing to take responsibility.

If this sort of behavior seems familiar, Lydia doesn't notice.

SCENE 17

Lydia's apartment.
Day 23.

KIMMIE is keyed up and anxious; she has some uncomfortable news to communicate. She worries the fabric of her poofy scarf.

Sorry, I'm a little hyper—things are just so...*tense*! *Every*where!

She stares intently at the scarf, twisting it in her hands.

So Lydia, I think that...well, I think that maybe you waited a little bit *too* long to come back to work.

(trying to put a sunny spin on it) I mean, I'm sure you can reapply, you know there are always openings, but...they had to give your job to someone else.

What is it about Kimmie, anyway?

Kimmie looks around nervously, her eyes landing on the camera.

Oh! I guess that was kind of *dramatic,* me telling you on the camera like that—I didn't even *plan* it that way!

I was just *thinking*—without being aware of the *video*—that I should tell you about what was going on with the whole job thing, first, before anything else, because—well—no one likes to be going into a situation *blind,* right?

But don't worry, Lydia, I know some of the managers at the other branches, and they're *really* really nice. And I bet they'd be *happy* to hire you! I mean, you'd have to start out at a lower *level* and everything, but you'd work your way *up!*

Kimmie smiles; she is really trying.

She fails.

Okay! So, oh no! I feel uncomfortable now. Sorry!

She looks at the camera. She's at a loss.

So what should I say?

Just talk? Okay...

But she doesn't.

Then something occurs to her.

Relieved to have something else to talk about, she plunges in:

Oh! So Kira—in new accounts?—told me this *morning* that she *saw you* at

Does Kimmie have more resilience, more perseverance, than Lydia? Does her relentless optimism give her some sort of sick advantage?

Will all the Lydias fall, surrendering their positions to the shiny Kimmies of the world?

And would that be the most fitting end to it all, anyway?

Leave the Lydias to their swamps of ambivalence and indecision, to the gloom and shadows of their doubt; invite the Kimmies to step forward, to advance with torches raised, to illuminate the world with their sunny outlooks?

a standup comedy open mic last week! Is that true?

That's so *funny*! That you're being *funny*! On *stage*! Or *trying* to be funny! And she said you were, um, (remembering the exact words) "Okay"! That you "weren't bad."

Well, that's better than being *bad*, right?

Oh, and you know what's so funny? Earlier this morning, before leaving for work, I saw, *your mom* on the Google National newsfeed! And I didn't know who she was at first, but then at the end of her report she was like, "This is Cynthia *Clark-Lin*," and I was like "Hey-hey-*hey*! So *that's* Lydia's mom!"

I'd never seen her before—you said she was only on the *Halifax* News feed and who watches *that*, right? People from Halifax, whatever, why would you download *their* news?

(catching herself: oops) I mean, no offense, Lydia, I *totally* don't think of you as being from Halifax—because you seem like such a San Francisco *native* now, yeah?

It was *so*, so-so-so *fun* seeing your mom, though. I wouldn't have noticed the resemblance, you know, because...

> She gestures toward Lydia's facial features, then quickly stops herself, realizing that this may not be the most appropriate thing to do. She moves on:

...But then when she said her name it just *totally*-totally *clicked*!

> She listens a moment.

ᒪ◦ ◦ ᑐ ᒪ ◖◖◦ᘓᣞ◦◦ᘓ ᐁ◦ᴕᔕ◖◦◦.◦.◦ᴗᴗ◦◦◦ ◦◦ᣞ ᴕ ᴕᴗᴕᴕᴕ◖◖◦ᴗ ◦◖ ◦ᴗᴗᴗᴗᴗᴗᴗᴗᴗᴕ◦ᴕᴗ◦ᴕᴗᴕᴗ◖ ᴗᴗᴗᴗᴗᴗ◦◦ ◦ ◦ᴕ ◦ ◦◦ ◖ᣞᴗᴗ◦

There is never a moment that doesn't count.

There are no free moments given, every act happens, every breath eats up oxygen, every minute takes up space in the space-time continuum.

No moment doesn't happen.

ACT TWO She was *good*, she was *really* good, as a newscaster. I *totally* believed everything she said, she was *very* commanding.

Hmm?

Oh, she was just talking...about something...going on...in Halifax...

(cheerfully giving up) I can never remember these things!

SCENE 18

Outside the Halifax FPMS unit.
Day 24.

BERNIE, suited up for work, walks over to her FPMS unit.

It is a quiet, early morning.

The sound of a gunshot.

Bernie crumples.

ᐃᐅᐸᑕ ᓄᓇᕗᑦ

doesn't   happen

SCENE 19

Outside the Halifax FPMS unit.
Some moments later.

From where Bernie has fallen, CYNTHIA rises slowly.

Her eyes take in what has happened.

Then, unsteady, she turns to look into the camera, delivering her report.

Local proponent for women's reproductive rights, Doctor Bernadette Tayag, was fatally shot through the skull by an unseen sniper as she entered her Family Planning Mobile Services unit in Halifax early this morning.

Born and raised in Halifax, California, Dr. Tayag had been an unwavering voice for abortion rights for years, and had become the public face of the new pro-choice movement.

A group called Halifaxans Organized to Respect Embryonic Sanctity has taken responsibility for the killing, which they say was justified in light of the current law governing abortion.

Regarded as a medical prodigy, Doctor Tayag was only thirty-two years old.

This is Cynthia Clark-Lin, reporting for *Greater Halifax News*.

END OF ACT TWO

ACT THREE

A FEW DAYS LATER;
A YEAR LATER.
DAYS 27 – END.

ACT THREE

SCENE 1

....

Lydia's apartment.
Day 27.

....

Lydia is holding Bernie's jacket.

As she sits, Lydia hears different voices—Bernie, Cynthia, Gin, Kimmie—swirling around her. She is remembering.

The voices crescendo, then stop abruptly.

She is alone.

LYDIA becomes aware of the camera.

She uses her own voice for the entirety of the scene, never "becoming" Bubbly or imitating Bubbly's voice.

There are no Bubbly lights. No Bubbly music plays.

ACT THREE

So.

I took both sets of pills.

Within the window.

I terminated the pregnancy.

And the night I took the first set of pills, Bubbly came to me.

I said, "Did you know about this all along? About Bernie? That this was going to happen? Do embryos just have a really sick sense of humor?"

And Bubbly says, "*I didn't know, Lydia.*"

And I say, "Are people going to do anything? Are they going to find who did it? Is it going to make the laws change back? Is her death going to mean anything."

And Bubbly says, "*I don't know, Lydia.*"

And I say, "Usually you know everything. You know everything, right? Now you don't know? Now you don't know anything? You can't explain this, or make it mean something?"

"Why am I doing this? You haven't even told me what I'm dying of."

And Bubbly doesn't say anything, just billows in and out of form.

Lydia waits a moment, staring at Bubbly, furious and lost.

"What am I dying of? Tell me."

And Bubbly says, *"I don't know, Lydia."*

"But I'm dying of something. I *am* dying, right?"

And Bubbly says...

She smiles as if she is just now realizing she was dumb enough to fall for the sickest, stupidest joke in the whole fucking world.

"...You will die eventually. Everyone does."

A moment as this lands.

"I'm not even dying? I don't have anything, like cancer, or a brain tumor, or something?"

(continuing, grim and deliberate) And Bubbly says, *"I'm not aware that you have anything, like cancer, or a brain tumor, or something."*

"Then why was I doing this? What was the point of all this, if I'm not even dying?"

And Bubbly begins to slowly break up, the bubbles falling away, dissolving before me into particles that drifted off, carried on some dream wind, scattering out across the vast distance.

And I was awake.

And I felt the blood leaving my body.

ACT THREE   And I thought of Bernie's blood leaving her body.

And I thought of invisible blood, everywhere, and invisible organs, and transplants, and obstacles.

(hating herself) **And I slept.**

> Lydia gets up and quietly turns the chair to face away from us.
>
> She hangs Bernie's jacket on the back of the chair.

SCENE 2

Cynthia's home.
Day 28.

CYNTHIA observes her daughter for some moments.

She seems to be about to say something several times before she
finally speaks.

Well I think it's horrible to be doing this, after what happened to
Bernadette. But I called you, Lydia, because I loved Bernadette. I loved
her very much.

And she told me, she told me this video, this was very important to you.

And you think you're dying, don't you.

(an attempt at humor) Well it looks like you were preparing for the *wrong* dying person!

    A failed attempt.

I'm *joking*, darling, don't get so worked up—you're going to work yourself into an early grave! (another attempt at humor) Even though you *don't work*!

    Another failed attempt.

(catching herself) I know, I'm sending you mixed signals.

And you've always been so funny about your name, Lydia, always telling me how you *found out* what it meant after I tried to *hide the truth from you* all these years.

I wasn't trying to *hide the truth* from you, Lydia. I just...didn't want to *tell* you about it. For my *own* reasons. How I came to your name had *nothing* to do with you—you didn't have to worry yourself over it.

And so imagine my surprise when you come to me, blathering away about how Lydians were the first people to mint coins in the sixth century B.C., and how Lydians were known for their fantastic wealth, and Lydians this and Lydians that—my god.

Well, I'll tell you a few things I was never planning on telling you, Lydia. Because sometimes, honestly, it feels as though we've reached the end of days.

And with Bernadette, what happened to her...

    Cynthia seems to be wrestling with how to say something.

I know you don't come to Halifax too often, stirs up bad memories of a miserable childhood I suppose, but Halifax is…

Well, it's a mess. And I'm reporting on it. But I think…

(firmly) I think it's best you stay out of Halifax, Lydia. It's too dangerous.

But I'll tell you, since we're reaching the End of Days: I kept your father's name, Lin, as part of mine, because I wanted…to keep something. Of him.

Well, of course I kept you, but you're *you*, you're not *mine*. I can't claim another individual as my property, or as part of my identity, as much as I would like to sometimes. People who think they can claim another person as their own…well, they're just setting themselves up for a fall, Lydia.

But your name…I'll tell you, it's a funny story.

And don't take it the wrong way.

Of course you *will*, because you take *every*thing the wrong way, you just can't help it, can you, Lydia…so *dramatic* all the time.

Let's see. My Lydia…

Cynthia chooses her words carefully, proceeding delicately.

Well the truth is, Lydia, that I named you…after a cow I once owned.

She eyes Lydia to gauge her reaction, then moves on quickly to explain.

You know I grew up on a dairy farm, and cows were for milking, and for

pets—not eating, beef was for eating—and that cow, Lydia, she was such a miracle.

I'd be up every morning at four o'clock to milk the rest of those stupid lowing things, Honestly, I loved them all, but Lydia was the strangest. She would always paw at the ground like one of those idiot horses that looks like it's doing math, but it's not really doing math, it's just trained to paw at the ground.

(with great fondness) Except Lydia wasn't trained to do any of that. She just found it comforting, to tap away at the ground. Tap, tap, tap. Tap-tap-tap. Just like that, the gesture. You know some people say a gesture is more unique than the person who executes it?

But in the end, that's what killed her.

Because there was a fire. And Lydia wouldn't stop tapping away at the ground. She was too attached to the repetition and the motion to run away and save herself.

So. Anyway. I named you in honor of Lydia the Cow.

And I can see the same thing happening to you, too, if you don't watch it, dear. Getting so obsessed with something that you don't even realize the barn is burning to ashes around you.

And then, you're dead.

She holds her gaze on Lydia a moment longer.

SCENE 3

....

The end of a clip.

....

BERNIE is sitting in the chair, her back facing the audience; the lighting is dreamy.

Maybe the apocalypse will come tomorrow, Lydia? Your problem is that you don't recognize an apocalypse when you see one.

I'm done with this. Turn that thing off. For real.

She waits.

It's still on, Lydia.

She waits.

(exploding) **Fine, leave it on. No one's gonna see this, anyway, because *you're not dying.***

After a moment of silence, Bernie closes her eyes, sighing.

Fuck. Sorry, Lydia.

She turns around in the chair, facing us.

Her anger is gone; she is thoughtful now.

You know, Lydia, I've been thinking…about growing up…in crazy little Halifax.

You know all that stuff, about the invisible blood, and the organs, and the dolls? I really really *believed* that shit. I don't know, maybe all those times, I *was* making *real* incisions somewhere…

You know, Lydia. This thing, your dreams?

I have to tell you—and I'm a doctor so you have to listen to me: nothing can be created or destroyed. It can just…transform. Everyone knows that, very basic physics stuff, right? So even though some people—including me, ordinarily, but I'm taking a step back from being professional Doctor Tayag here for a minute so I can tell you this—even though *some* people might say, "Oh, you terminated it, it's over, it's gone, it's behind you"— No, not really, Lydia. It's not like that, I don't think.

I think that now…it's just a *part* of you.

So maybe those dreams can go away, if you just remember that, yeah?

Bernie smiles.

Lydia stands, picks up Bernie's jacket, and puts it on.

She takes the remote control and points it at the camera:

Click.

The lights dim.

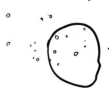

SCENE 4

A coffee shop or performance spot somewhere.
A year later.

LYDIA is at the microphone, mid-set.

So I've been thinking about destiny a lot, lately. Big questions. Like, what am I doing here, anyway?

And what are *you* doing here? My god, it's your Friday night. I mean, *I'm* good, I'm getting paid.

Well, not really, but I thought you might think more highly of me, if you thought I was getting paid.

I used to think my destiny was to work with monetary units. Because I've always, you know, dreamed big. Ambition isn't for everyone. Don't judge.

But as it turns out, all this time my destiny has apparently been to burn to death in a barn as a dim-witted yet charismatic land mammal with no survival instinct. Thanks, Mom.

My best friend, people call her the "Death Angel," because she, you know, kills babies and stuff. And I've always kind of envied her for that. Because you've never really lived until you've been accused of the mass murder of infants.

I'm kidding, she doesn't kill babies. She used to. But all that's behind her now—she's dead. She died a year ago actually. But I always wanted to tell that joke when she was still alive. One thing I've learned through all of this is that you should never put off publicly mocking someone you care about, because if you wait too long, they could die. And then you can't use the joke anymore. Unless you use it in really bad taste, like what I just did.

My mother and I got to help scatter her ashes—that was fun. Really great mother-daughter bonding activity, I highly recommend it to anyone looking for some intensely awkward alone time with an estranged family member. It was a windy day, so the ashes got picked up and carried on the currents, it was quite lovely. And then the wind shifted, so...still lovely, but also, you know, dusty.

I've started getting along better with my mother lately. I think it's because, as I get older, I really start to...forget my childhood.

I'm kidding. I haven't forgotten anything. But I wanted her to think I had. So she wouldn't see it coming.

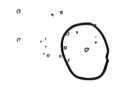

I moved back in with my mother recently. That's what she gets for naming me after a cow. It's cute, we've already established our routine: she insults me, cries, and tells me some happy anecdote from childhood that I don't remember; and I let her insult me, cry, and tell me some happy anecdote from childhood that I don't remember. And then I use it in my routine.

It's a vicious cycle.

I hate it when people say, "Well, if insert-dead-person's-name were here, she or he would say, insert-some-jocular-yet-profound-considering-the-circumstances remark."

But I think I'm gonna do it anyway. I think if Bernie were here, she'd say, "What the fuck? I can't believe I'm dead. Well, you'd better make sure my death wasn't in vain or I'm haunting the fuck out of you worthless living pieces of shit. I will abort you from beyond the grave."

(lifting up her hand holding an imaginary gun, firing) *Backa-backa*!

But she'd say it with love.

I can't exactly take up Bernie's mantle and become a doctor; I think enough innocent life has already been lost—and I'm not talking about the innocent embryos or the innocent fetuses, okay? Please. Those embryos had it coming.

But I can at least talk about her and stuff. And it's good to get out here like this, and be together, and communicate in some way. To see each other. To talk. Because, who knows. Maybe the apocalypse will come tomorrow.

Well, that's my time. Thanks for, um, listening.

Good night.

END OF PLAY

A FEW NOTES

The world of *Lydia's Funeral Video* is one in which regressive laws concerning women's reproductive rights are only one feature in a larger (and bleaker) landscape. In this world, corporations dominate and more conservative attitudes toward individual freedoms prevail.

But as the gentle reader has likely already noted, a world in which corporations dominate and more conservative attitudes prevail doesn't sound all that different from the country some of us live in now; Lydia's world, a not-so-distant future San Francisco, does closely resemble our own world, but with a few critical adjustments.[1]

Lydia's San Francisco features a more robust level of corporate presence (Bernie alludes to "world rule by Verizon and Facespace"); climate change has become more severe (tornadoes are touching down regularly in Alaska); the United States is entangled in even more wars (in Iran and North Korea); employers have increased control over monitoring their employees and clients (every account holder at Chase is required to get an optical scan); right-wing groups nonchalantly publicize and pursue legally questionable tactics in service of their extremist ideology (Lindsey Gough announces on live television her organization's plans to hunt down abortion providers); and, most prominently in the context of this story, Planned Parenthood has closed its doors, and women in the United States can get abortions only from for-profit ventures like Bernie's FPMS, or from an underground network of unlicensed providers who prowl online avenues like Craigslist.[2]

....

1. For a ballpark location of this book's "now", please refer to the copyright date.

2. A world in which the most reliable and visible provider of women's reproductive services is forced to close its doors less than a century after opening them is depressingly easy to imagine. In the 1980s, Planned Parenthood endured a period in which patients and providers were frequently stalked and intimidated, and clinics were targets of arson and bombings. Today, the organization is regularly battling legislative attacks to eliminate funding or block participation in public health programs. *LFV*, then, takes place in a world that both recalls the past and extrapolates into the future: a landscape of intimidation and terror that is even further along that what we've seen before, and that is in many ways sanctioned by the government.

I began writing *LFV* in the fall of 2007 in part as a response to what I perceived to be a heightening and sharpening of more regressive attitudes: the Supreme Court had recently upheld a ban on a form of late term abortion,[3] suggesting that revisiting *Roe v. Wade* was a possibility (as well as paternalistically reasoning that the ban would protect women who would inevitably come to regret their abortions[4]); there was a renewed surge in ballot initiatives designed to undo some of the gains made decades earlier (one representative initiative in Colorado proposed to recognize a fertilized egg as a "person" entitled to "inalienable rights, equality of justice, and due process of law" under the state constitution[5]); and, culturally, there was a proliferation of movies celebrating the unintended pregnancy (*Knocked Up, Juno, Waitress*), where abortion was never seriously considered—they may not have been planning for a baby, but a baby (with all its crazy, wacky ramifications!) was what they were gonna get.[6] While these stories are certainly lovely and worthy on their own, together (and in the absence of any alternative mainstream narratives) I felt they were obscuring and silencing more complex realities.

Setting this story in the not-so-distant future offered the opportunity to integrate both existing, "actual" conditions as well as extrapolations and exaggerations of existing conditions. The effect, for me, is a hybrid world that throws into doubt what is "real" and what isn't; a viewer might know that we're *obviously* not in a world where women are getting abortions in repurposed military tanks; but *are* we in a world where tornadoes are touching down in Alaska? (Since, actually, they are, but how frequently?) And what exactly is the current legal cutoff date for abortions? (It varies from state to state, but which is the most liberal, and most restrictive?) The not-so-distant future setting establishes an ambiguity that prompts us to question where and when we are, and to question what is actually happening right now. The play is suffused with a sense of uncertainty.

Which makes sense, since this is a story about uncertainty: a story that involves an unintended pregnancy, but one in which the birth of a child is not the presumed and uncontested conclusion.

....

3. *Gonzales v. Carhart*. The form of abortion in question is known by medical providers as intact dilation and evacuation, but more widely known as the "partial birth" abortion, a term given it by its critics.

4. In a *Slate* article, Dahlia Lithwick described the decision as "less about the scope of abortion regulation than an announcement of an astonishing new test: Hereinafter, on the morally and legally thorny question of abortion, the proposed rule should be weighed against the gauzy sensitivities of that iconic literary creature: the Inconstant Female."

5. The movement toward winning these sorts of "rights" for zygotes generally and irritatingly calls itself the Personhood Movement. At the time, similar ballot initiatives were also underway in several other states, including Montana, Georgia, Oregon, Michigan, and South Carolina. Such initiatives are still regularly being introduced across the country at this time.

6. Writing about the 2008 Dark Room production of *LFV* for KQED's Arts & Culture Blog, Claire Light described these films as "unintended-pregnancy-fests." Light went on to observe how these films shape the social and political conversation: "[T]hrough the medium of politically regressive Hollywood flicks, we discover that the range of choice for battered wives, single mothers, and teenagers now spans keeping the kid (joyfully) or (tearfully) playing cornfield for a barren couple. We're taught that it's bad to say the 'A' word (and offered the high-larious 'schmushmortion' in its place), and asked to believe that women for whom abortion might be the best financial and emotional choice, would simply pass it up without thought, discussion, or process."

I was interested in the absolute gray area of such a situation, and in characters who wrestle with the ambiguity and complexity of their circumstances. For Lydia, even if she ultimately decides to terminate her pregnancy, the choice is never clear or easy.

ʊ ̈ʊ

THE PRODUCTIONS

The play version of *Lydia's Funeral Video* developed over the course of various productions and workshops.

The first production took place at San Francisco's Dark Room Theater and was directed by Wilma Bonet, whose vision and spirit coaxed the first expression of the play into being. (She also generously hosted several rehearsals in her home, and went above and beyond the directorial call of duty by journeying to Ikea in Emeryville to find what would become the Bubbly lights.) Wilma and I worked closely together with the designers to explore and discover the sound, look, and texture of the show. The sound designer and composer was Kendall Li, who created all the musical themes and sound cues, including the themes for Bubbly and the faux-country of Lydia, and, of course, the epic *Greater Halifax News* music. The costume designer was Gail Baugh, who created striking, convertible costume pieces that facilitated the transformation between and realization of multiple characters.

In August 2008, Tom Connors directed a second full production at the CSV Milagro Theater as part of the New York International Fringe Festival. Tom made critical contributions to the play's development, including pointing out structural issues, encouraging further edits and adjustments in the script, and pushing us to find new takes on various characters.

Later presentations included a full performance at the Marsh (as part of the Marsh Rising series), and a workshop production at Columbia University, directed by Ashley Kelly-Tata. Ashley championed a reimagining of the show, experimenting with an on-stage camera and live video feed to flesh out and inform the piece.

Individuals who contributed to the productions and workshops:

THE 2008 SAN FRANCISCO DARK ROOM PRODUCTION
Wilma Bonet, director
Kendall Li, composer and sound designer/engineer
Gail Baugh, costume designer
Mark Baugh-Sasaki, set designer
Derek Chung, graphic designer and photographer
Kendall Li, Aaron Niles, Josh Johnson, lights/sound ops
Jim Espinas & Ian Johnson, videographer
Interviewees: Claire Light, Mika Ashlee Sasaki, Christina Patton, Sita Bhaumik, and others

Workshop participants: Dan Weil, Elokin Orton, Han Pham, Sita Bhaumik, Sadie Contini, Mark Baugh-Sasaki, Claire Light, Jim Espinas, Kendall Li, Chuck Lacson, Gary Chou
Co-presenters: MANJA, Prime Image Media Group, Many Threads, Asian American Theater Company, and Locus Arts
Supported by a Cultural Equity Grant from the San Francisco Arts Commission

THE 2008 FRINGENYC PRODUCTION
Thomas Connors, director
Daniel Tien Simon, authorized company representative
Anton Delfino & Whitney Mosery, lights/sound ops
Sam Crow, videographer

THE 2010 COLUMBIA UNIVERSITY WORKSHOP PRODUCTION
Ashley-Kelly Tata, director
Michelle Cote, stage manager
Rich Song, videographer

THE BOOK

Special thanks to Spoon+Fork co-founder and designer Chez Bryan Ong, who patiently and gamely conceived numerous drafts of the book's layout and design over the course of the project, and whose genius realized the final (and thirty-first!), multilayered version.

Illustrator and artist Matt Huynh created the images accompanying the text. We asked Matt to watch a video of a live performance of the play, and to make free-associative doodles throughout—train of consciousness drawings. The result was the series of doodles—sometimes playful, sometimes disturbing, and often both—that now occupy various spaces in the book and on the cover.

We are indebted to visual artist Jenifer Wofford, who had attended the original production in San Francisco, and who worked with us during a significant early period when we were first exploring the imagery and how it might function. Her participation and contributions were critical in developing some of the visual ideas for the book.

OTHER THANKS & ACKNOWLEDGEMENTS

In addition to those acknowledged above who participated in the production and development of the play, this project owes its beingness to many other humans who have generously lent their insights, expertise, time, energy, support, patience, and all around brilliance at various stages along the way.

Claire Light, who introduced *Lydia's Funeral Video* to Kaya.

The amazing, tenacious crew at Kaya and at Spoon+Fork: Neelanjana Banerjee, Jennifer Chou, Jean Ho, Pritsana Kootint-Hadiatmodjo, Zoë Ruiz, Lydia Tam, Jolene Torr, Patty Wakida, and Ann Tomoko Yamamoto.

Kaya publisher and editor Sunyoung Lee, who not only tirelessly and heroically supported this project over the years with her invaluable guidance and advice, but whose crazy wisdom fundamentally shaped this book by originating the ideas for the counterpoint narrative and illustrations; also, who judiciously pushed me through very many necessary rewrites of the script, CPN, essays, and other sections (including this one).

And other dear and honored folks who also offered invaluable feedback and support throughout: Sita Bhaumik, May Briosos, Jocelyn Burrell, Kevin B. Chen, Darryl Chiang, Derek Chung, Sadie Contini, Clarence Coo, Jim Espinas, Glenn Fajardo, Jewelle Gomez, Kel Haney, Brandon Haynes, Selena Hsu, Melissa Hung, Jane Kim, Goh Nakamura, Chuck Lacson, Robert Lee, Ebony McKinney, Andrea Merrett, Shizue Seigel & Benjamin Pease, Malayka Rios, Daniel Tien Simon, Robynn Takayama, Michelle Talgarow, Thy Tran, Laura Valdez, Han Wang, Dan Weil, San San Wong, Duncan Williams, Jenifer Wofford, Don Wood, Bryan Wu, Luna Yasui; anyone I've unintentionally left out (and with my deepest apologies); my parents, Kai and Doris Chanse; my sisters, Catherine, Ursula, and Vikki; and fellow fleshbot/izakaya comrade/bicoastal champion, Jon.

And to my friends and family who have patiently listened to me agonizing over this book at various points over the last half-decade: I owe you all a drink.

AFTERWORD
EYE CONTACT

You're painfully shy as a kid. Your face flushes red when you have to speak in class, and you're filled with panic. You fear the judgment of others. A lot. You don't want to get in trouble. You're scared and want everyone to like you and think you're good. You can't even look people in the eye.

So, naturally, you want to be on stage.

It starts in first grade, in a play about two kites. You play the breeze. You wear a pink leotard and a scarf and you don't have many lines. But you get to hang out on stage being *the breeze* and your face doesn't flush red and you're not embarrassed being there. (This is a few years before you decide you hate pink and know you will never wear it again, which is a few half-decades before you realize that pink's not so bad, just an alternate shade of burgundy, really, and burgundy's awesome, so what's the issue?)

You land your first big role in eighth grade, when you're cast as Tuc in *Mother Hicks*. Tuc is the quasi-narrator, the faithful companion of the lead character, and, also, a deaf mute. Even though playing Tuc doesn't involve the actual use of vocal chords, there are a fair number of signed lines, and it feels like a weighty, important role. During your free periods, you get coached in sign language by a girl two years older than you, Stacey Chung, a sophomore, which makes you feel sort of special. Stacey Chung is Chinese American, which means something to you on some subconscious level, since almost everyone else in your school is white, but you're in eighth grade and your Asian American identity/consciousness is in its super-embryonic stages. Also, you're still mostly unaware of your own internalized racism, so the slight aversion you have to Stacey Chung, tied to the sense of having a special connection with her, is for the most part underacknowledged and completely uninvestigated.

(Probably, in some remote corner of your brain/spirit/soul, it occurs to you that you, one of three Asian American girls in your class, is playing the deaf mute character, and that maybe there might be some broader implications to all that, but it occurs to you in a not particularly useful or articulate way. Besides, you've got like sixteen long speeches to learn in sign language, not to mention a few random wild gesticulations and deaf-mute blocking—who's got time to wrestle with all this other complicated, murky bullshit?)

The play is about some wayward white girl who winds up running away and living with a medicine woman of sorts, the titular Mother Hicks of the play, who has been shunned by her conservative small town, and is considered a witch. (She's also played by one of three Latina girls in the class.) "*Mother Hicks is a witch, people say,*" you sign, as the rest of the cast says it out loud so the audience knows what the deaf-mute character is saying. (You, Tuc, don't think Mother Hicks is a witch; you're her only loyal companion. But you're letting the audience know what the ignorant townsfolk think. Things go bad? Blame Mother Hicks.)

Tuc is the only character in the play who talks directly to the audience, which means *you* have to talk directly to the audience. Except you can't *really* talk directly to the audience, because you can't actually *make eye contact* with anyone in the audience. What if you looked at someone's face, and saw that she was bored, or annoyed, or hated you? And you ended up forgetting your lines and your blocking, and the play was ruined? Way to fuck up the eighth-grade spring production, asshole.

So you train yourself to look at the tops of people's heads, instead. This seems like a solid way to *not* look directly at people's faces and freak you out, while still getting the angle *close* enough so audience members will *think* you're looking at them, and will feel recognized and connected to. Win-win. You feel pretty good about yourself for innovating such a sophisticated, cutting-edge performance technique.

For the play, you wear enormous overalls you find at an outlet store in your mother's homeland of Pennsylvania, where there are many cheap outlet stores, and no sales tax.

(You wear baggy clothes a lot. You think it's a cool anti-girly-girl fashion choice, but probably you're just insecure and want to hide yourself. While being on stage crying out for attention at the same time. Ah, the paradox!)

You pull off the whole no-eye-contact thing, and the play is well received. Rave reviews for your giant-overalls-clad deaf-mute! You are exhilarated by the terrific success of the eighth-grade production of *Mother Hicks*, and you write impetuously in your journal that if you can't be an actor *you will kill yourself*.

(Three years later, when your identity/consciousness is a bit more developed and you're one of the co-chairs of an Asian American student group, you confront the director of that play—a teacher you love, the head of the tiny drama department at your school—pointing out that he always casts the blonde white girls in the lead female roles, and the students of color as the other significant, but not lead romantic, roles. You are rewarded for your bold, honest critique, you think, by being cast in *The Tempest* the following year, your senior year in high school, as the hapless, love-struck Miranda, a terrifically boring role that you also happen to suck at. Apparently, there's not much resonance between you and Young Lover characters.)

Fast forward (through some spectacularly unspectacular years of depression, going to school, switching schools, leaving school, going back to school, going out West and back East and out West again) to San Francisco, the early-to-mid aughts. After having stopped acting for some time, you've picked it up again, and are performing in short pieces that you write with a small Filipino American theater called Bindlestiff Studio. You've even joined their Pinay theater collective. You can't claim to be Filipina (much less the way cooler *pinay*), but you pass, and no one seems too pissed about your being there in all your non-pinayness. Every show, you're doing the whole tops of heads thing; it's really working out well for you.

At this point you don't have a choice; you've been conditioning yourself to do it for years now. The very idea of actually looking directly into someone's face and making eye contact while performing on stage triggers a wave of primal, gut terror. You don't know what exactly you might see in those faces—boredom, contempt, even interest—but whatever it is, you don't want to deal with it.

A few people at the theater do standup, which is something you would never do—you imagine it must be totally embarrassing and painful, the worst position you could possibly put yourself in as a performer. (You have never heard of the work of artists such as, for instance, Marina Abramovic, so your bar for "worst position" is admittedly pretty low. Still, given what you know, standup comedy seems like an awful, horrible thing to do.)

So you decide to sign up for a standup comedy class.

It's more as a dare, you think. Sure it'll be embarrassing and painful, but you figure it'll stretch your writing and performance muscles, and, while being embarrassing and painful, also be, ultimately, character building.

You find, to your surprise, that you actually enjoy the class. It's fun coming up with bits, and you even (totally humbly) think you've got a keen eye for recognizing the absurd foibles of humans and society. Ha ha! You are totally a natural at this! Your observations of human nature, race, class, and politics are brilliant and incisive!

You notice your instructor (artist-performer-human of legend Allan Manalo) makes eye contact a lot, but surely *you* won't have to do that; you do the tops-of-heads things during class exercises, and continue with the workshop.

The first public standup set you do is in a small, narrow bar in the Mission, dark inside on a bright Saturday afternoon. There are a handful of people there, lounging around with a drink. Most of them seem to be looking at you, wondering what you're doing there.

Your name is called, and you approach the mic stand. You glance out but don't look directly at anyone's face. You gather, from what you pick up in your peripheral, that people are assessing you, wondering what you're doing there. And probably, quietly, hating you.

You begin. Your first bit is explaining your ethnicity: *My mom is Pennsylvania Dutch—half Swiss, half German—and my dad is Chinese—but thinks he's white—so that makes me, hmm, roughly three-quarters?...fucked up.* Some laughter, not much. You're glancing around, not at anyone in particular, looking at the tops of heads. The tops-of-heads approach, it is quickly becoming apparent, has some drawbacks in a tiny, narrow bar; people can clearly see you're not looking at them. You know it, but there's nothing you can do about it.

You continue with your set, explaining your last name—*"Chanse," spelled C-H-A-N-S-E. It's not a very common name*—you can already feel how bored everyone is—*because my dad made it up*—a stray chuckle or two, as you cast your eyes to another part of the room, hoping to convey the sense of being engaged with the audience— *and he did that because when he first moved to this country he experienced some racism*—this is ridiculous, you have to look at people—*so when he started having kids*—as the terror spikes, you look at a man leaning against the bar with a drink in his glass—*he changed our last name from "Chang" to "Chanse"*—just before meeting his eyes, you're certain you can feel the contempt radiating from him—*to protect us*—you make eye contact—*so people wouldn't knoooow*—what? the man's smiling, listening— *that we were part Chinese*. The man at the bar laughs. You are looking right at one another. You glance a few bar stools down, at a woman. She's not laughing, she looks vaguely bored, and it doesn't feel so awful to see that. When your eyes meet hers, her expression shifts. She sort of smiles.

You suddenly understand the most obvious thing in the world: you can't do this thing if you aren't connecting directly to the people you're in the room with. You need to look them in the eye.

The rest of that set goes fine. You continue doing standup for a few years, while also writing and performing theater. Some sets are good, even great, some are *eh*, some are terrible. Often you do look out into the sea of faces, and the eyes you happen to meet *are* filled with what could reasonably be described as genuine contempt. But there are other emotions you think you encounter, too: interest, confusion, enjoyment, boredom, curiosity, impatience, or something completely neutral or otherwise indecipherable. But whatever sort of expression you meet, whatever seems to be behind those eyes, you still look.

You don't see it this way immediately, but you do feel the relief, and the exhilaration, of suddenly understanding it's okay; that you don't need to go around reflexively defending yourself against the judgment of others.

You don't see it this way immediately, but you begin to understand that you can't control the way people respond to you, not really, but it's important to be there in the room with other people, no matter how they respond.

You don't see it this way immediately, but you begin to understand that the principle of making and holding eye contact while doing standup can be applied to doing theater— that theater is facilitating a lived, immediate experience that connects people in time and space. It is a union of minds and bodies and souls in a unique moment.

You don't see it this way immediately, but you begin to understand that the principle of eye contact while doing standup can be applied not only to theater but to living, that we are here to be with others, to be present, to not look away; we are here to pay attention.

You remember hearing somewhere that attention is a form of love.

You think about how this idea of attention and eye contact is what performance boils down to. That when you're talking about making a solo performance piece, eye contact and attention and being in the room with others is an integral part of the process. Exposing yourself and making yourself vulnerable is part of the process. Risking and inviting the judgment of others is part of the process.

You think about how even if there are only two or three people in the room, you need to have that idea of eye contact. Not in the literal sense, but in the sense of experiencing a direct, embodied connection.

And, many years later, when you are working through (and throwing out) draft after draft of an essay, trying to come up with an even remotely intelligible approach to introducing (or afterwording) a printed version of a play, you think about how making a book is a form of making eye contact. It is about exposing yourself, making yourself vulnerable by offering this connection.

Over half a decade ago, when I was starting to think about what would become *Lydia's Funeral Video*, I knew that writing a Play About Abortion (and especially a Play About Abortion And Also About My Own Abortion) was something I would never do. I felt it would be maudlin, overly self-absorbed, and that ultimately I would be doing a disservice to whatever questions I was interested in exploring.

So I avoided it for a long time, and then wrote it anyway.

I've come to realize that writing and performing this play, and now this book, have been me making eye contact all along; this is what making any piece of theater or art is, at some fundamental level: exposing yourself; risking judgment, shame, failure; making yourself vulnerable in an effort to connect to the world. It's training your gaze down, down from the tops of heads, until, at last, you find someone's eyes gazing back.

PORTRAIT BY EUGENE PARK based on a PHOTOGRAPH BY DEREK CHUNG

SAM CHANSE

Sam Chanse is a writer and theater artist
based in New York and California. A
2015 Sundance Ucross Playwright Fellow
and member of the Ma-Yi Writers Lab,
her work has also been supported by the
Lark Play Development Center, Labyrinth
Theater, Leviathan Lab, the Actor's Studio
Playwrights/Directors Unit, Second
Generation, Ars Nova, Bindlestiff Studio,
Asian American Theater Company, Tofte
Lake Center, and the San Francisco Arts
Commission. She received her MFA in
playwriting from Columbia University, and
in musical theater writing from NYU's Tisch
School of the Arts. For some years in the
aughts, she served as the artistic director of
San Francisco-based arts nonprofit Kearny
Street Workshop, and as co-director of
Locus Arts. A former & proud member of
bantercut, she is also a fan of the biocoastal
salon sensation that is Laundry Party.